JOSEPH SMITH

AS

SCIENTIST

A CONTRIBUTION TO
MORMON PHILOSOPHY

BY

John A. Widtsoe, A. M., Ph. D.

THE GENERAL BOARD
YOUNG MEN'S MUTUAL IMPROVEMENT
ASSOCIATIONS
SALT LAKE CITY, UTAH
1908

Preface

In the life of every person, who receives a higher education, in or out of schools, there is a time when there seems to be opposition between science and religion; between man-made and God-made knowledge. The struggle for reconciliation between the contending forces is not an easy one. It cuts deep into the soul and usually leaves scars that ache while life endures. There are thousands of young people in the Church to-day, and hundreds of thousands throughout the world, who are struggling to set themselves right with the God above and the world about them. It is for these young people, primarily, that the following chapters have been written.

This volume is based on the conviction that there is no real difference between science and religion. The great, fundamental laws of the Universe are foundation stones in religion as well as in science. The principle that matter is indestructible belongs as much to theology as to geology. The theology which rests upon the few basic laws of nature is unshakable; and the great theology of the future will be such a one.

"Mormonism" teaches and has taught from the beginning that all knowledge must be included in the true theology. Because of its comprehensive philosophy, "Mormonism" will survive all religious disturbances and become the system of religious faith which all men may accept without yielding the least part of the knowledge of nature as discovered in the laboratories or in the fields. The splendid conceptions of "Mormonism" concerning man and nature, and man's place in nature are among the strongest testimonies of the divine nature of the work founded by Joseph Smith, the Prophet.

This little volume does not pretend to be a complete treatment of "Mormon" philosophy; it is only a small contribution to the subject. There is room for elaboration and extension in this field for many generations to come. The attempt has been made to sketch, briefly, the relation of "Mormonism" to some features of modern scientific philosopy, and to show that not only do "Mormonism" and science harmonize; but that "Mormónism" is abreast of the most modern of the established views of science, and that it has held them many years—in some cases before science adopted them. The only excuse for the scant treatment of such an important subject is that it is as extensive as the duties of a busy life would allow. In the future, the subject may be given a fuller treatment.

Some readers may urge that "the testimony of the Spirit," which has been the final refuge of so many Christians, has received little consideration in the following chapters. This is due to the avowed purpose of the work to harmonize science and religion, on the basis of accepted science. "Mormonism" is deeply and rationally spiritual; the discussion in this volume is confined to one phase of Gospel philosophy.

The majority of the following chapters were originally published in the *Improvement Era* for 1903-1904 as a series of articles bearing the main title of this book. These articles are here republished with occasonal changes and additions. The new chapters have been cast into the same form as the original articles. The publication as independent articles will explain the apparent lack of connection between the chapters in this book. The statements of scientific facts have been compared very carefully with standard authorities. However, in popularizing science there is always the danger that the simplification may suggest ideas that are not wholly accurate. Those who have tried this kind of work will understand and pardon such errors as may appear. However, corrections are invited.

My thanks are due and cheerfully given the management of the *Improvement Era* for the help and encouragement given. I am under especial obligations to Elder Edward H. Anderson, the associate editor of the *Era*, to whose efforts it is largely due that this volume has seen the light of day. I desire to render my thanks also to the committee appointed by the First Presidency to read the manuscript, Elders George Albert Smith, Edward H. Anderson and Joseph F. Smith, Jr.

This volume has been written in behalf of "Mormonism." May God speed the truth!

Contents.

Chapter I.

JOSEPH'S MISSION AND LANGUAGE.

The mission of Joseph Smith was of a spiritual nature; and therefore, it is not to be expected that **Scientific discussions not to be expected in the Prophet's work.** the discussion of scientific matters will be found in the Prophet's writings. The revelations given to the Prophet deal almost exclusively with the elucidation of so-called religious doctrines, and with such difficulties as arose from time to time in the organization of the Church. It is only, as it appears to us, in an incidental way that other matters, not strictly of a religious nature, are mentioned in the revelations. However, the Church teaches that all human knowledge and all the laws of nature are part of its religious system; but that some principles are of more importance than others in man's progress to eternal salvation.* While on the one hand, therefore, it can-

---

* "And truth is knowledge of things as they are, and as they were and as they are to come."—Doctrine and Covenants, 93: 24.

"Teach ye diligently and my grace shall attend you, that you may be instructed more perfectly in theory, in principle, in doctrine, in the law of the Gospel, in all things that pertain unto the Kingdom of God, that are expedient for you to understand;

"Of things both in heaven and in the earth, and under

not reasonably be expected that Joseph Smith should deal in his writings with any subject peculiar to natural science, yet, on the other hand, it should not surprise any student to find that the Prophet at times considered matters that do not come under the ordinary definition of religion, especially if they in any way may be connected with the laws of religion. Statements of scientific detail should not be looked for in Joseph Smith's writings, though these are not wholly wanting; but rather, we should expect to find

---

the earth, things which have been, things which are, things which must shortly come to pass; things which are at home, things which are abroad; the wars and the perplexities of the nations, and the judgments which are on the land, and a knowledge also of countries and kingdoms,

"That ye may be prepared in all things when I shall send you again to magnify the calling, whereunto I have called you, and the mission with which I have commissioned you."—Doctrine and Covenants, 88: 78-80.

And verily, I say unto you, that it is my will that you should hasten to translate my Scriptures, and to obtain a knowledge of history, and of countries, and of kingdoms, of laws of God and man, and all this for the salvation of Zion."—Doctrine and Covenants, 93: 53.

"It (theology) is the science of all other sciences and useful arts, being in fact the very foundation from which they emanate. It includes philosophy, astronomy, history, mathematics, geography, languages, the science of letters, and blends the knowledge of all matters of fact, in every branch of art and research......All that is useful, great and good, all that is calculated to sustain, comfort, instruct, edify, purify, refine or exalt intelligences, originated by this science, and this science alone, all other sciences being but branches growing out of this, the root."—Pratt, Key to Theology, chap, 1.

general views of the relations of the forces of the universe.

It is not in harmony with the Gospel spirit that God, except in special cases, should reveal things

Man must not expect direct revelation in matters that he can solve for himself.

that man by the aid of his natural powers may gain for himself. The Lord spoke to the Prophet as follows:— " Behold, you have not understood; you have supposed that I would give it unto you, when you took no thought, save it was to ask me; but, behold, I say unto you, that you must study it out in your mind; then you must ask me if it be right, and if it is right I will cause that your bosom shall burn within you; therefore, you shall feel that it is right.''* Such a doctrine makes it unreasonable to look to the Prophet's work for a gratuitous mass of scientific or other details, which will relieve man of the labor of searching out for himself nature's laws. So well established is this principle that in all probability many of the deepest truths contained in the writings of Joseph Smith will not be clearly understood, even by his followers, until, by the laborious methods of mortality, the same truths are established. It is even so with the principles to be discussed in the following papers. They were stated seventy years ago, yet it is only recently that the Latter-day Saints have begun to realize that they are identical with recently developed scientific truths; and the world of science is not yet aware of it. However, whenever such harmony is observed, it testifies of the divine inspiration of the humble, unlearned boy prophet of the nineteenth century.

---

*Doctrine and Covenants 9: 7, 8.

The Prophet Joseph does not use the language of science; which is additional proof that he did not know the science of his day. This may be urged as an objection to the assertion that he understood fundamental scientific truths, but the error of this view is easily comprehended when it is recalled that the language of science is made by men, and varies very often from age to age, and from country to country. Besides, the God who spoke to Joseph Smith, says, "These commandments were given unto my servants in their weakness, after the manner of their language, that they might come to understanding."* If God had spoken the special language of science, the unlearned Joseph Smith would not, perhaps, have understood. Every wise man explains that which he knows in the language of those to whom he is speaking, and the facts and theories of science can be quite easily expressed in the language of the common man. It is needless to expect scientific phraselogy in the writings of Joseph Smith.

The absence of the language, details and methods of science in the Prophet's writings proves him unfamiliar with the written science of his day.

Scientific details are almost wholly wanting in the writings of Joseph Smith. Had the Prophet known the science of his day, his detailed knowledge would have been incorporated somehow in his writings. The almost complete absence of such scientific detail as would in all probability have been used, had the Prophet known of it, is additional testimony that he did not get his information from books.

Finally, another important fact must be mentioned. Men in all ages have speculated about the

---

* Doctrine and Covenants 1:24.

things of the universe, and have invented all kinds of theories to explain natural phenomena. In all cases, however, these theories have been supported by experimental evidence, or else they have been proposed simply as personal opinions. Joseph Smith, on the contrary, laid no claim to experimental data to support the theories which he proposed, nor did he say that they were simply personal opinions, but he repeatedly asserted that God had revealed the truths to him, and that they could not, therefore, be false. If doctrines resting upon such a claim can be shown to be true, it is additional testimony of the truth of the Prophet's work.

In the following chapters it will be shown, by a series of comparisons, that, in 1833, or soon there-**Purpose of the following chapters.** after, the teachings of Joseph Smith, the Mormon Prophet, were in full harmony with the most advanced scientific thought of today, and that he anticipated the world of science in the statement of fundamental facts and theories of physics, chemistry, astronomy and biology.

Chapter II.

THE INDESTRUCTIBILITY OF MATTER.

It was believed by the philosophers of ancient and mediaeval times, especially by those devoted to the study of alchemy, that it was possible through mystical powers, often of a supernatural order, to annihilate matter or to create it from nothing. Men with such powers transcended all known laws of nature, and became objects of fear, often of worship to the masses of mankind. Naturally enough, the systems of religion became colored with the philosophical doctrines of the timés; and it was held to be a fundamental religious truth that God created the world from nothing. Certainly, God could do what his creatures, the magicians, were able to do— that part of the reasoning was sound.

Until recent days many believed that matter could be created or destroyed.

In support of this doctrine, attention was called to some of the experiences of daily life. A piece of coal placed in a stove, in a short time disappears— it is annihilated. From the clear air of a summer's day raindrops start—created out of nothing. A fragment of gold placed in contact with sufficiently strong acids, disappears—it is destroyed.

Towards the end of the eighteenth century, facts

and laws of chemistry were discovered, which enabled scientists to follow in great detail the changes, visible or invisible, to
which matter in its various forms is
subject. Then it was shown. that the

Matter is eternal, its form only can be changed.

coal placed in a stove unites with a portion of the
air entering through the drafts, and becomes an invisible gas, but that, were this gas collected as it
issues from the chimney, it would be found to contain a weight of the elements of the coal just equal
to the weight of the coal used. In a similar manner
it was shown that the raindrops are formed from the
water found in the air, as an invisible vapor. The
gold dissolved in the acid, may be wholly recovered
so that every particle is accounted for. Numerous
investigations on this subject were made by the most
skillful experimenters of the age, all of which
showed that it is absolutely impossible to create or
destroy the smallest particle of matter; that the most
man can do is to change the form in which matter
exists.

After this truth had been demonstrated, it was
a necessary conclusion that matter is eternal, and that
the quantity of matter in the universe cannot be
diminished nor increased. This great generalization,
known as the law of the Persistence of Matter or
Mass, is the foundation stone of modern science. It
began to find general acceptance among men about
the time of Joseph Smith's birth, though many religious sects still hold that God, as the Supreme Ruler,
is able at will to create matter from nothing. The
establishment of this law marked also the final down-
fall of alchemy and other kindred occult absurdities.

No doctrine taught by Joseph Smith is better understood by his followers than that matter in its

Mormonism teaches that all things are material. elementary condition is eternal, and that it can neither be increased nor diminished. As early as May, 1833, the Prophet declared that "the elements are eternal,"[*] and in a sermon delivered in April, 1844, he said " Element had an existence from the time God had. The pure principles of element are principles which can never be destroyed; they may be organized and reorganized, but not destroyed. They had no beginning, and can have no end."[†]

It is thus evident that from the beginning of his work, Joseph Smith was in perfect harmony with the fundamental doctrine of science; and far in advance of the religious sects of the world, which are, even at this time, slowly accepting the doctrine of the persistence of matter in a spiritual as well as in a material sense.

Mormonism has frequently been charged with accepting the doctrine of materialism. In one sense, the followers of Joseph Smith plead yes to this charge. In Mormon theology there is no place for immateralism; i. e. for a God, spirits and angels that are not material. Spirit is only a refined form of matter. It is beyond the mind of man to conceive of an immaterial thing. On the other hand, Joseph Smith did not teach that the kind of tangible matter, which impresses our mortal senses, is the kind of matter which is associated with heavenly beings. The distinction between the matter known to man

---

[*] Doctrine and Covenants, 93: 33.

[†] The Contributor, Vol. 4, p. 257.

and the spirit matter is very great; but no greater than is the difference between the matter of the known elements and that of the universal ether which forms one of the accepted dogmas of science.

Science knows phenomena only as they are associated with matter; Mormonism does the same.

Chapter III.

THE INDESTRUCTIBILITY OF ENERGY.

It is only when matter is in motion, or in the possession of energy, that it is able to impress our senses. The law of the indestructibility and convertibility of energy, is of equal fundamental value with that of the indestructibility of matter.

All forms of energy may be converted into each other. Energy can not be destroyed.

A great variety of forces exist in nature, as, for instance, gravitation, electricity, chemical affinity, heat and light. These forces may all be made to do work. Energy, in fact, may be defined as the power of doing work. In early days these forces were supposed to be distinct and not convertible, one into the other, just as gold and silver, with our present knowledge, are distinct and not convertible into other elements.

In the early part of the nineteenth century students of light and heat began to demonstrate that these two natural forces were different manifestations of one universal medium. This in turn led to the thought that possibly these forces, instead of being absolutely distinct, could be converted one into the other. This idea was confirmed in various experimental ways. Sir Humphrey Davy, about the end of the eighteenth century, rubbed together two pieces of ice until they were nearly melted. Precautions had been taken that no heat could be abstracted from the outside by the ice. The only tenable conclusion was that the energy expended in rubbing, had been converted into heat, which had melted the ice. About the same time, Count Rumford, a distinguished American, was superintending the boring of a cannon at the arsenal at Munich, and was forcibly struck with the heating of the iron due to this process. He, like Davy, believed that the energy of the boring instruments had been converted into the heat.*

From 1843 to 1849, Dr. Joule of Manchester, England, published the results of experiments on the relation between mechanical energy and heat. Dr. Joule attached a fixed weight to a string which was passed over a pulley, while the other end was connected with paddles moving in water. As the weight descended, the paddles were caused to revolve; and it was observed that, as the weight fell and the paddles revolved, the water became warmer and warmer. Dr. Joule found further that for each foot of fall, the same amount of heat energy was given to the water. In fact, he determined that when a pound weight falls seven hundred and seventy two feet it gives out energy enough to raise the temperature of one pound of water one degree Fahrenheit.† This experiment, frequently repeated, gave the same result and established largely the law of the convertibility of energy.

About the same time, it was shown that light can be converted into heat; and later it was proved that electricity may be changed into heat or light. In all these cases it was found that the amount of energy changed was exactly equal to the amount of energy produced.

---

* The Conservation of Heat—Stewart, pp. 38, 39.

† The Conservatism of Energy—Stewart, pp. 44, 45. Recent Advances in Pysical Science—Tait, pp. 63, 65,

Thus, by countless experiments, it was finally determined that energy is indestructible; that, when any form of energy disappears, it reappears immediately in another form. This is the law of the persistence of force or energy. In more recent days, it has been suggested that all known forces are variations of a great universal force, which may or may not be known. The very nature of force or energy is not understood. In the language of Spencer, "By the persistence of force, we really mean the persistence of some cause which transcends our knowledge and conception."[*]

It need hardly be explained that energy cannot exist independently of matter; and that the law of the persistence of matter is necessary for the existence of the law of persistence of force.

Joseph Smith was not a scientist; and he made no pretense of solving the scientific questions of this

Universal Intelligence, comparable to universal energy is indestructible, according to Joseph Smith. day. The discussion relative to the convertibility of various forms of energy was in all probability not known to him. Still, in his writings is found a doctrine which in all respects resembles that of the conservation of energy.

Joseph Smith taught, and the Church now teaches, that all space is filled with a subtle, though material substance of wonderful properties, by which all natural phenomena are controlled. This substance is known as the Holy Spirit. Its most important characteristic is intelligence. "Its inherent properties embrace all the attributes of intelligence."[†]

---

[*] First Principles, Spencer, 4th ed., p. 200.

[†] Key to Theology, P. P. Pratt, 5th ed., p. 40.

The property of intelligence is to the Holy Spirit what energy is to the gross material of our senses.

In one of the generally accepted works of the Church, the energy of nature is actually said to be the workings of the Holy Spirit. The passage reads as follows: "Man observes a universal energy in nature—organization and disorganization succeed each other—the thunders roll through the heavens; the earth trembles and becomes broken by earthquakes; fires consume cities and forests; the waters accumulate, flow over their usual bounds, and cause destruction of life and property; the worlds perform their revolutions in space with a velocity and power incomprehensible to man, and he, covered with a veil of darkness, calls this universal energy, God, when it is the workings of his Spirit, the obedient agent of his power, the wonder-working and life-giving principle in all nature."*

In short, the writings of the Church clearly indicate that the various forces of nature, the energy of nature, are only manifestations of the great, pervading force of intelligence. We do not understand the real nature of intelligence any better than we understand the true nature of energy. We only know that by energy or intelligence gross matter is brought within reach of our senses.

Intelligence or energy was declared by Joseph Smith in May, 1833, to be eternal: "Intelligence, or the light of truth, was not created or made, neither indeed can be."† In the sermon already referred to

---

* Compedium, Richards and Little, 3rd ed., p. 150.

† Doctrine and Covenants, 93: 29.

the Prophet said, "The intelligence of spirits had no beginning, neither will it have an end."

These quotations, and many others to which attention might be called, show clearly that Joseph Smith taught the doctrine that the energy of the universe can in nowise be increased or diminished, though, it may manifest itself in various forms.

The great Latter-day prophet is thus shown to be in harmony with the second fundamental law of science. It is not a valid objection to this conclusion to say that Joseph Smith did not use the accepted terms of science. Words stand only for ideas; the ideas are essential. The nomenclature of a science is often different in different lands, and is often changed as knowledge grows.

It is hardly correct to say that he was in harmony with the law; the law as stated by the world of science was rather in harmony with him. Let it be observed that Joseph Smith enunciated the principle of the conservation of the energy, or intelligence as he called it, of the universe, in May, 1833, ten years before Dr. Joule published his famous papers on energy relations, and fifteen or twenty years before the doctrine was clearly understood and generally accepted by the learned of the world. Let it be also remembered that the unlearned boy from the backwoods of New York state, taught with the conviction of absolute certainty that the doctrine was true, for God had revealed it to him.

If God did not reveal it to him, where did he learn it, and whence came the courage to teach it as an eternal truth?

Chapter IV.

THE UNIVERSAL ETHER.

The nature of light has been in every age a fascinating subject for study and reflection. Descartes,

The modern theory of light was established only about the year 1830. the French mathematician and philosopher, advanced the hypothesis that light consists of small particles emitted by luminous bodies, and that the sensation of light is produced by the impact of these particles upon the retina of the eye. Soon after this emission or corpuscular theory had been proposed, Hooke, an English investigator of great note, stated publicly that the phenomena of light, as he had observed them, led him to the belief that the nature of light could best be explained on the assumption that light was a kind of undulation or wave in some unknown medium, and that the sensation of light was produced when these waves struck upon the retina of the eye. This new hypothesis, known as the theory of undulations, after the great Isaac Newton had declared himself in favor of the corpuscular theory, was finaly adjudged by the majority of students to be erroneous.

About the year 1800, more than a century after the days of Descartes, Hooke and Newton, an English physician, Dr. Thomas Young, who had long experimented on the nature of light, asserted that the emission theory could not explain many of the best known phenomena of light. Dr. Young further claimed that correct explanations could be made only by the theory of waves of undulation of an etherial medium diffused through space, and presented numerous experimental evidences in favor of this view. This revival of the old theory of undulation met at first with violent opposition from many of the greatest scientific minds of the day. Sometime after Dr. Young's publication, a French army officer, Augustine Fresnel, undertook the study of the nature of light, and arrived, almost independently, at the conclusion stated by Dr. Young. Later, other investigators discovered light phenomena which could be explained only on the undulatory hypothesis, and so, little by little, the new theory gained ground and adherents.

Still, even as late as 1827, the astronomer Herschel published a treatise on light, in which he appeared to hold the real merit of the theory of undulations in grave doubt.* Likewise, the Imperial Academy at St. Petersburg, in 1826, proposed a prize for the best attempt to relieve the undulatory theory of light of some of the main objections against it.† It was several years later before the great majority of the scientific world accepted the .theory of undulatons as the correct explanation of the phenomena of light.

In brief, this theory assumes that a very attenuated, but very elastic, substance, called the ether, fills all space, and is found surrounding the ultimate

---

.* History of the Inductive Sciences, Whewell, 3rd edition, Vol. II, p. 114.

† Loc. cit., 117.

particles of matter. Thus, the pores of wood, soil,
lead, gold and the human body, are
**A subtle sub-
stance, the ether,** filled with the ether. It is quite impos-
fills all space. sible by any known process to obtain
a portion of space free from it. A luminous body is
one in which the ultimate particles of matter, the
atoms or molecules, are moving very rapidly, and
thus causing disturbances in the ether, similar to the
disturbances in quiet water when a rock is thrown
into it; and, like the water wave, proceeding from
the point of disturbance, so the ether waves radiate
from the luminous body into space. When a wave
strikes the retina of the eye, the sensation of light is
produced. This new-found ether was soon used for
the explanation of other natural phenomena.

The nature of heat had long been discussed
when the world of science decided in favor of the
Light, heat, undulatory theory of light. One school
**electricity and
other forces are** held that the sensation of heat was
forms of ether caused by the cannonading of heat
motion. particles by the heated body; the other
school, with few adherents, insisted that heat was
simply a form of motion of the ether already adopted
in the theory of light. The later discoveries of
science proved with considerable certainty that the
undulatory theory of heat is right, but it was well
towards the middle of the last century before the
emission theory of heat lost its ground. In fact, Dr.
Whewell, in the third edition of his classic book on
the *History of Inductive Sciences*, published in 1859,
says that the undulatory theory of heat "has not by
any means received full confirmation;" and Dr.

---

* Vol. II, p. 184.

John Tyndall, in a book published in 1880, says, that the emission theory "held its ground until quite recently among the chemists of our own day."[*] Today, the evidences of modern science are overwhelmingly in favor of the undulatory theory of heat.

The wonderful developments of the last century, in electricity and magnetism, led to much speculation concerning the nature of the subtle electrical and magnetic forces. The most popular theories for many years were those that presupposed various electrical and magnetic fluids, which could be collected, conducted, dispersed and otherwise controlled. In 1867, the eminent English mathematician, Clerk Maxwell, proposed the theory that electrical and magnetic phenomena were simply peculiar motions of the ether, bearing definite relationship to light waves. Later researches, one result of which is the now famous Roentgen or X-rays, have tended to confirm Maxwell's theory. A recent text-book on physics, of unquestioned authority,[†] states that the ether theory of electricity and magnetism is now susceptible of direct demonstration; and another eminent authority frankly states that "when we explain the nature of electricity, we explain it by a motion of the luminiferous ether."[‡]

Other recent discoveries have hinted at the possibility of matter itself being only the result of peculiar forms of this all-pervading substance, the luminiferous ether. The properties of the element radium,

---

[*] Heat, A Mode of Motion, Tyndall, 6th ed., p. 38.

[†] Lehrbuch der Physik, Riecke,(1896), 2ter Band, p. 315.

[‡]Popular Lectures and Addresses, Kelvin (1891) Vol. 1, page 334.

and other radioactive elements, as at present understood, suggest the possibility of a better understanding of the nature of the ether, and of its relation to the world of phenomena.

That the present knowledge of the world of science compels a faith in an all-pervading substance,
The existence of the ether is a certainty of science. of marvelous properties, and of intimate relationship to all forms of energy, is shown by the following quotations from Lord Kelvin, who is generally regarded as the world's greatest physicist: "The luminiferous ether, that is the only substance we are confident of in dynamics. One thing we are sure of, and that is the reality and substantiality of the luminiferous ether." "What can this luminiferous ether be? It is something that the planets move through with the greatest ease. It permeates our air; it is nearly in the same condition, so far as our means of judging are concerned, in our air and in the interplanetary space." "You may regard the existence of the luminiferous ether as a reality of science." "It is matter prodigiously less dense than air—of such density as not to produce the slightest resistance to any body going through it."*

The theory of the ether is one of the most helpful assumptions of modern science. By its aid the laws of energy have been revealed. There is at the present time no grander or more fundamental doctrine in science than that of the ether. The nature of the ether is, of course, far from being clearly understood, but every discovery in science demonstrates that the hypothetical ether stands for an im-

* Kelvin's Lectures, Vol. 1, pp. 317, 334, 336, 354.

portant reality of nature.   Together with the doctrines of the indestructibility of matter and energy,
the doctrine of the ether welds and explains all the
physical phenomena of the universe.

Joseph Smith, in a revelation received on De-
cember 27, 1832, wrote:

"The light which now shineth, which giveth
you light, is through him who enlighteneth your
eyes, which is the same light that
quickeneth your understandings; which
light proceedeth forth from the presence of God to fill the immensity of
space. The light which is in all things:
which is the law by which all things are governed:
even the power of God."*

Joseph Smith taught space is filled with a substance comparable to the ether of science.

This quotation gives undoubted evidence of the
prophet's belief that space is filled with some substance which bears important relations to all natural phenomena.   The word substance is used ad-
visedly; for in various places in the writings of
Joseph Smith, light, used as above in a general
sense, means spirit,† and "all spirit is matter, but
it is more fine and pure."‡

True, the passage above quoted does not fur-
nish detailed explanation of the Prophet's view concerning the substance filling all space, but it must
be remembered that it is simply an incidental paragraph in a chapter of religious instruction. True,
also, the Prophet goes farther than some modern
scientists, when he says that this universal substance

---

* Doctrine and Covenants, section 88: 11-13.

† Doctrine and Covenants, 84: 45.

‡ Ibid, 131: 7.

bears a controlling relation to all things; yet, when it is recalled that eminent, sober students have suggested that the facts of science make it possible to believe that matter itself is simply a phenomenon of the universal ether, the statement of the "Mormon" prophet seems very reasonable. The paragraph already quoted is not an accidental arrangement of words suggesting an idea not intended by the prophet, for in other places, he presents the idea of an omnipresent substance binding all things together. For instance, in speaking of the controlling power of the universe he says:

"He comprehendeth all things, and all things are before him, and all things are round about him; and he is above all things, and in all things, and is through all things, and is round about all things."*

That Joseph Smith does not here have in mind an omnipresent God, is proved by the emphatic doctrine that God is personal and cannot be everywhere present.†

Lest it be thought that the words are forced, for argument's sake, to give the desired meaning, it may be well to examine the views of some of the persons to whom the Prophet explained in detail the meanings of the statements in the revelations which he claimed to have received from God.

Parley P. Pratt, who, as a member of the first quorum of apostles, had every opportunity of obtaining the Prophet's views on any subject, wrote

* Ibid, 88: 41.

† Ibid, 130: 22.

in considerable fullness on the subject of the Holy
Spirit, or the light of truth:

"As the mind passes the boundaries of the visible world, and enters upon the confines of the more
refined and subtle elements, it finds itself associated
with certain substances in themselves invisible to
our gross organs, but clearly manifested to our intellect by their tangible operations and effects."
"The purest, most refined and subtle of all these
substances—is that substance called the Holy Spirit."
"It is omnipresent." "It is in its less refined particles, the physical light which reflects from the sun,
moon and stars, and other substances; and by reflection on the eye makes visible the truths of the
outward world."*

Elder C .W. Penrose, an accepted writer on
Mormon doctrine, writes, "It is by His Holy Spirit,
which permeates all things, and is the life and light
of all things, that Deity is everywhere present. * *
By that agency God sees and knows and governs all
things."†

Such quotations, from the men intimately associated or acquainted with the early history of the
Church, prove that Joseph Smith taught in clearness
the doctrine that a subtle form of matter, call it
ether or Holy Spirit, pervades all space; that all
phenomena of nature, including, specifically, heat,
light and electricity, are definitely connected with
this substance. He taught much else concerning this
substance which science will soon discover, but

---

* Key to Theology, 5th ed., pp. 38-41.

† Rays of Living Light, No. 2, p. 3.

which lies without the province of this paper to discuss.

By the doctrine of the ether, it is made evident all the happenings in the universe are indelibly inscribed upon the record of nature. A word is spoken. The air movements that it causes disturbs the ether. The ether waves radiate into space and can never die. Anywhere, with the proper instrument, one of the waves may be captured, and the spoken word read. That is the simple method of wireless telegraphy. It is thus that all our actions shall be known on the last great day. By the ether, or the Holy Spirit as named by the Prophet, God holds all things in His keeping. His intelligent will radiates into space, to touch whomsoever it desires. He who is tuned aright can read the message, flashed across the ether ocean, by the Almighty. Thus, also, God, who is a person, filling only a portion of space is, by His power carried by the ether, everywhere present.

The ether of science though material is essentially different from the matter composing the elements. So, also, in Mormon theology, is the Holy Spirit different from the grosser elements. In science there is a vast distinction between the world of the elements, and that of the ether; in theology, there is an equally great difference between the spiritual and material worlds. Though the theology of Joseph Smith insists that immaterialism is an absurdity, yet it permits no overlapping of the earthly and the spiritual.

It must not be overlooked that the broad statement of this doctrine was made by Joseph Smith,

Joseph Smith stated the existence of a universe-filling substance before science had generally accepted it. at least as early as 1832, at a time when the explanation of light phenomena on the hypothesis of a universal ether was just beginning to find currency among learned men; and many years before the same hypothesis was accepted in explaining the phenomena of heat and electricity.

The idea of an influence pervading the universe is not of itself new. Poets and philosophers of all ages have suggested it in a vague, hesitating manner, without connecting it with the phenomena of nature, but burdening it with the greatest absurdity of religion or philosophy, that of immaterialism. Joseph Smith said the doctrine had been taught him by God, and gave it to the world unhesitatingly and rationally. The men of science, to whom Joseph Smith appears only as an imposter, and who know nothing of his writings, have later discovered the truth for themselves, and incorporated it in their books of learning.

Had Joseph Smith been the clever imposter that some claim he was, he probably would not have dealt in any way with the theories of the material world, at least would not have claimed revelations laying down physical laws; had he been the stupid fool, others tell us he was, his mind would not have worried itself with the fundamental problems of nature.

However that may be, it is certain that Joseph Smith, in the broad and rational statement of the existence of an omnipresent, material though subtle substance, anticipated the workers in science.   In view of that fact, it is not improbable that at some future time, when science shall have gained a wider view, the historian of the physical sciences will say that Joseph Smith, the clear-sighted, first stated correctly the fundamental physical doctrine of the universal ether.

Chapter V.

THE REIGN OF LAW.

In the seventh book of the *Republic of Plato**
occurs the following passage:

"Imagine a number of men living in an underground cavernous chamber, with an entrance open
The realities of nature are known by their effects. to the light, extending along the entire
length of the cavern, in which they
have been confined, from childhood,
with their legs and necks so shackled, that they are
obliged to sit still and look straight forward, because
their chains render it impossible for them to turn
their heads round; and imagine a bright fire burning some way off, above and behind them, and an
elevated roadway passing between the fire and the
prisoners, with a low wall built along it, like the
screens which conjurers put up in front of their audiences, and above which they exhibit their wonders. Also figure to yourself a number of persons
walking behind the wall, and carrying with them
statues of men and images of other animals,
wrought in wood and stone and all kinds of materials, together with various other articles, which
overtop the wall; and, as you might expect, let some
of the passers-by be talking, and the others silent.

"Let me ask whether persons so confined could
have seen anything of themselves or of each other,
beyond the shadows thrown by the fire upon the part

---

* Golden Treasury edition, pp. 235, 236.

of the cavern facing them? And is not their knowledge of the things carried past them equally limited? And if they were able to converse with one another, would they not be in the habit of giving names to the objects which they saw before them? If their prison house returned an echo from the part facing them, whenever one of the passers-by opened his lips, to what could they refer the voice, if not to the shadow which was passing? Surely such person would hold the shadows of those manufactured articles to be the only realities.''

With reference to our absolute knowledge of the phenomena of nature, this splendid comparison is as correct today as it was in the days of Plato, about 400 B. C.; we are only as prisoners in a great cave, watching shadows of passing objects thrown upon the cavern wall, and reflecting upon the real natures of the things whose shadows we see. We know things only by their effects; the essential nature of matter, ether and energy is far from our understanding.

In early and mediaeval times, the recognition of the fact that nature in its ultimate form is unknowable, led to many harmful superstitions. **The progress of science rests on the law of cause and effect.** Chief among the fallacies of the early ages was the belief that God at will could, and did, cause various phenomena to appear in nature, which were contrary to all human experience. As observed in chapter 4, a class of men arose who claimed to be in possession of knowledge which made them also able, at will, to cause various supernatural manifestations. Thus arose the occult sciences, so called,—alchemy, astrology, magic, witchcraft, and all other similar abominations of the intellect. Such beliefs made the logical study of nature superfluous, for any apparent regularity or law in nature might at any time be overturned by a person in possession of a formula of the black art or a properly treated broomstick.

While such ideas prevailed among the majority of men, the rational study of science could make little progress. In the march of the ages as the ideas of men were classified, it began to be understood that the claims of the devotees of the mystical arts not only could not be substantiated but were in direct opposition to the known operations of nature. It became clear to the truthseekers, that in nature a given cause, acting upon any given object, providing all surrounding conditions be left unchanged, will always produce the same effect. Thus, coal of a certain quality, brought to a high temperature in the presence of air, will burn and produce heat; a stick held in water at the right angle will appear crooked; iron kept in contact with moisture and air, at the right temperature, will be changed into rust; sunlight passed through a glass prism will be broken into rainbow colors; ordinary plants placed in a dark cellar will languish and die. No matter how often trials are made, the above results are obtained; and today it is safe to assert that in the material world no relation of cause and effect, once established, has failed to reappear at the will of the investigator. As this principle of the constancy in the relations between cause and effect was established, the element of chance in natural phenomena, with its attendant arts of magic, had to disappear. It is now well understood by intelligent persons that the law of order controls all the elements of nature.

It is true that the cause of any given effect may, itself, be the effect of other causes, and that the first cause of daily phenomena is not and probably cannot be understood. It is also true that very seldom is the mind able to comprehend why certain causes, save the simpler ones, should produce certain effects. In that respect we are again nothing more than Plato's cave prisoners, seeing the shadows of ultimate realities. However, the recognition of the principle of the invariable relation between cause and effect was a great onward stride in the intellectual development of the world.

Now, as men began to investigate nature with her forces, according to the new light, numerous relations of the forces were discovered— in number far beyond the comprehension of the human mind. Then it was found necessary to group all facts of a similar nature, and invent, if possible, some means by which the properties of the whole group might be stated in language so simple as to reach the understanding. Thus came the laws of nature.

Laws of nature are man's simplest expression of many related facts.

For instance, men from earliest times observed the heavenly bodies and the regularity of their motions. Theories of the universe were invented which should harmonize with the known facts. As new facts were discovered, the theories had to be changed and extended. First it was believed that the earth was fixed in mid-space, and sun and stars were daily carried around it. Hipparchus improved this theory by placing the earth not exactly in the center of the sun's circle. Ptolemy, three hundred years later, considered that the sun and moon move in circles, yearly, around the earth, and the other planets in circles, whose centers again described circles round the earth. Copernicus simplified the whole system by teaching that the earth rotated around its axis, and around the sun. Keppler next showed that the earth moved around the sun in certain curves termed ellipses. Finally, Newton hit upon the wide-embracing law of gravitation, which unifies all the known facts of astronomy.* All the earlier laws were correct, so far as they included all the knowledge of the age in which they were proposed, but were insufficient to include the new discoveries.

Laws of nature are, therefore, man's simplest and most comprehensive expression of his knowledge of certain groups of natural phenomena. They are man-made, and subject to change as knowledge grows; but, as they change, they approach or should approach more and more nearly to the perfect law. Modern science is built upon the assumption that the relations between cause and effect are invariable, and that these relations may be grouped to form great natural laws, which express the modes by which the forces of the universe manifest themselves.

In this matter, science is frankly humble, and acknowledges that the region of the unknown is far greater than that of the known. Forces, relations and laws may exist as yet unknown to the world of science, which, used by a human or superhuman be-

---

* See The Grammar of Science, Pearson, pp. 117, 118.

ing, might to all appearances change well-established

A miracle is a law not understood. relations of known forces. That would be a miracle; but a miracle simply means a phenomenon not understood, in its cause and effect relations. It must also be admitted that men possess no absolute certainty that though certain forces, brought into a certain conjunction a thousand times, have produced the same effect, they will continue to do so. Should a variation occur, however, that also must be ascribed to an inherent property of the forces or conditions, or the existence of a law not understood.* There can be no chance in the operations of nature. This is a universe of law and order.

Were it not for the sake of the completeness of the argument running through these chapters, it would

Joseph Smith taught the Invariable relation of cause and effect. be unnecessary to call attention to the fact that Joseph Smith in a very high degree held views similar to those taught by science relative to cause and effect, and the reign of law.

From the beginning of his career, the Prophet insisted upon order, or system, as the first law in the religion or system of philosophy which he founded.† Moreover, the order which he taught was of an unchangeable nature, corresponding to the invariable relation between cause and effect. He wrote, " There is a law, irrevocably decreed in heaven before the foundations of this world, upon which all blessings are predicated; and when we obtain any blessing

---

* The Credentials of Science, the Warrant of Faith, Cooke, pp. 169, 170.

† Doctrine and Covenants, 28: 13; 132; 8.

from God, it is by obedience to that law upon which it is predicated.''* No text book in science has a clearer or more positive statement than this, of the fact that like causes have like effects, like actions like results. The eternal nature of natural law is further emphasized as follows:

'' If there be bounds set to the heavens, or to the seas: or to the dry land, or to the sun, moon or stars; all the times of their revolutions; all the appointed days, months, and years, and all the days of their days, months, and years, and all their glories, laws, and set times, shall be revealed, in the days of the dispensation of the fullness of times, according to that which was ordained in the midst of the Council of the Eternal God of all other Gods before this world was.''†

Those who may be inclined to believe that this doctrine was taught in a spiritual sense only, should recall that Joseph Smith taught also that spirit is only a pure form of matter,‡ so that the principles of the material world must have their counterparts in the spiritual world. Besides, in the last quotation reference is made to such material bodies as sun, moon, and stars. In other places, special mention is made of the fact that the material universe is controlled by law. For instance:

''All kingdoms have a law given: and there are many kingdoms; * * * * and unto every kingdom is given a law; and unto every law there are certain bounds also and conditions. * * * *

* Doctrine and Covenants, 130: 20, 21.

† Doctrine and Covenants, 121: 30-32.

‡ Doctrine and Covenants, 131: 7.

And again, verily I say unto you, he hath given a law unto all things by which they move in their times and their seasons; and their courses are fixed; even the courses of the heavens and the earth, which comprehend the earth and all the planets.[*]

This also is a clear, concise statement of law and its nature, which is not excelled by the definitions of science. There can be no doubt from these quotations, as from many others that might be made, that Joseph Smith based his teachings upon the recognition that law pervades the universe, and that none can transcend law. In the material world or in the domain of ether or spirit, like causes produced like effects—the reign of law is supreme.

Certainly the claim cannot be made that Joseph Smith anticipated the world of science in the recognition of this important principle; but it is a source of marvel that he should so clearly recognize and state it, at a time when many religious sects and philosophical creeds chose to assume that natural laws could be set aside easily by mystical methods that might be acquired by anyone. In some respects, the scientific test of the divine inspiration of Joseph Smith lies here. Ignorant and superstitious as his enemies say he was, the mystical would have attracted him greatly, and he would have played for his own interest upon the superstitious fears of his followers. Instead, he taught doctrines absolutely free from mysticism, and built a system of religion in which the invariable relation of cause and effect is the cornerstone. Instead of priding himself, to his

"The law also maketh you free."

[*] Doctrine and Covenants, 88:36-38, 42, 43.

disciples, upon his superiority to the laws of nature, he taught distinctly that "the law also maketh you free."* Herein he recognized another great principle—that freedom consists in the adaptation to law, not in the opposition to it.

However, whatever else the Prophet Joseph Smith was, he most certainly was in full harmony with the scientific principle that the universe is controlled by law.

* Doctrine and Covenants, 98:8.

Chapter VI.

THE NEW ASTRONOMY.

From the dawn of written history, when the first men, watching through the nights, observed the

The laws of the motions of the heavenly bodies have been learned very slowly. regular motions of the moon and stars, humanity has been striving to obtain a correct understanding of the relation of the earth to the heavenly obdies.

First it was believed that the sun, moon, and stars revolved in circles around the earth (which for a time was supposed to be flat instead of spherical). The great Greek philosopher, Hipparchus, after observing the movements of the heavenly bodies, suggested that the earth was not exactly in the middle of the circles. Three hundred years later, Ptolemy discovered a number of facts concerning the movements of the sun, moon and planets, which were unknown to Hipparchus, and which led him to suggest that the sun and moon move in circles around the earth, but that the planets move around the earth in circles, whose centres again move around the earth. This somewhat complex theory explained very well what was known of astronomy in the days of the ancients. In fact, the views of Ptolemy were quite generally accepted for 1300 years.

About 1500, A. D., Copernicus, a Dutch astronomer, having still more facts in his possession than had Ptolemy, concluded that the simplest manner in which the apparent movements of the sun, moon, and planets could be explained, was to assume that the sun is the center of the planetary system, and that the earth, with the moon and planets, revolves according to definite laws around the sun. This theory, supported by numerous confirmatory observations, was generally accepted by astronomers, and really did explain very simply and clearly many of the facts of planetary motion.

Fifty years after the death of Copernicus, the celebrated astronomer, Kepler, proposed extensions and improvements of the Copernican doctrine, which made the theory that the planets revolve about the sun more probable than ever before. He suggested first that the planets move around the sun in closed curves, resembling flattened circles, and known as ellipses. By assuming this to be true, and assisted by other discoveries, he was also able to state the times required by the planets for their revolutions around the sun, and the velocity of their motions at different times of the year. Later investigations have proved the great laws proposed by Copernicus and Kepler to be true; and from their days is dated the birth of modern astronomy.

After the laws of the motions of the planets had been determined, it was only natural that men **The law of gravitation is universal and explains many of the motions of celestial bodies.** should ask themselves what forces were concerned in these motions. The ancient philosophers had proposed the idea that the sun attracts all heavenly bodies, but the suggestion had not been accepted by the world at large. However, after the discoveries of Kepler, the English philosopher Newton advanced the theory that there is in the universe an attractive force which influences all matter, beyond the limits of known space. He further proved that the intensity of this force varies directly with the product of the attractive masses, and inversely, with the square of the distances between them—that is, the greater the bodies the greater the attraction; the greater the distance between them, the smaller the attraction. This law of gravitation has been verified by repeated experiments, and, taken in connection with the astronomical theories of Copernicus and Kepler, has made celestial mechanics what they are today.

By the aid of the law of gravitation, many astronomical predictions have been fulfilled. Among the most famous is the following incident:

In the early part of the last century, astronomers noticed that the motions of the planet Uranus did not agree with those derived from calculations based upon the law of gravitation. About 1846, two investigators, M. Leverrier, of France, and Mr. Adams of England, stated, as their opinion, that the discordance between theory and observation in the case of the motions of Uranus, was due to the attraction of a planet, not yet known, and they calculated by means of the law of gravitation, the size and orbit of the unknown planet. In the fall of 1846, this planet was actually discovered and named Neptune. It was found to harmonize with the predictions made by the astronomers before its discovery.

During the days of Newton, the question was

raised if the celestial bodies outside of the solar system obey the law of gravitation. Among the stars, there are some which are called double stars, and which consist of two stars so near to each other that the telescope alone can separate them to the eye. In 1803, after twenty years of observation, William Herschel discovered that some of these couples were revolving around each other with various angular velocities. The son of William Herschel continued this work, and many years later, he discovered that the laws of motion of these double stars are the same as those that prevail in the the solar system.* This result indicated not only the universality of the law of gravitation, but also the probability that all heavenly bodies are in motion.

Then, early in the nineteenth cetury, a new method of research began to be developed, which was

The invention of the spectroscope laid the foundation of the new astronomy. destined to form a new science of astronomy. It had long been known that white light when passed through a glass prism is broken into a colored spectrum, with colors similar to those observed in the rainbow. Now it was discovered that when white light passes through vapors of certain composition, dark lines appear in the spectrum, and that the position of the lines varies with the chemical composition of the vapors. By the application of these principles, it was shown, towards the middle of the last century, that the chemical composition of the heavenly bodies may be determined. Later,

---

* History of the Inductive Sciences, Whewell, 3rd ed. Vol. I, pp. 467-469.

it was discovered that by noting the positions of the dark lines in the spectrum, it could be known when a star or any heavenly body is moving, as also the direction and amount of its motion. These unexpected discoveries led to a study of the heavens from the spectroscopic point of view, which has resulted in a marvelous advance in the science of astronomy.

It has been determined that all heavenly bodies are in motion, and that their velocities are great **All heavenly bodies are in motion.** compared with our ordinary conceptions of motion. Most of the stars move at the rate of about seven miles per second, though some have a velocity of forty-five miles, or more, per second. Many stars, formerly thought to be single, have been resolved into two or more components. The rings of Saturn have been proved to consist of small bodies revolving about the planet in obedience to Kepler's law.* Clusters of stars have been found that move through space as one body, as possible counterparts of the planetary system.† It has been demonstrated, further, that the sun itself, with its planets, is moving through space at a very rapid rate. Professor Simon Newcomb, perhaps the greatest astronomer of the day, says, "The sun, and the whole solar system with it, have been speeding their way toward the star of which I speak (Alpha Lyrae) on a journey of which we know neither the beginning nor the end. During every

---

* See C. G. Abbott, Report of Smithsonian Institution, for 1901, pp. 153-155.

† Light Science for Leisure Hours, Proctor, pp. 42-52.

clock-beat through which humanity has existed, it has moved on this journey by an amount which we cannot specify more exactly than to say that it is probably between five and nine miles per second. The conclusion seems unavoidable that a number of stars are moving with a speed such that the attraction of all the bodies of the universe could never stop them."[*]   In brief, the new astronomy holds that all heavenly bodies are in motion, and that the planetary system is but a small cluster of stars among the host of heaven. Further, it has weighed the stars, measured the intensity of their light, and determined their chemical composition, and it affirms that there are suns in the heavens, far excelling our sun in size and lustre, though built of approximately the same elements.

Sir Robert Ball expresses his views as follows: "The group to which our sun belongs is a limited one. This must be so, even though the group included all the stars in the milky way. This unnumbered host is still only a cluster, occupying, comparatively speaking, an expressibly small extent in the ocean of infinite space. The imagination will carry us further still —it will show us that our star cluster may be but a unit in a cluster of an order still higher, so that a yet higher possibility of movement is suggested for our astonishment."[†]

The solar system is only one of many.

Another eminent astronomer expresses the same idea briefly but eloquently: "It is true that from

---

[*] The Problems of Astronomy, S. Newcomb, Science, May 21. 1897.

[†] The Story of the Sun, R. S. Ball, pp. 360, 361.

the highest point of view the sun is only one of a multitude—a single star among millions—thousands of which, most likely, exceed him in brightness, magnitude and power. He is only a private in the host of heaven."[*]

And still another student of the stars propounds the following questions: "Does there exist a central sun of the universe? Do the worlds of Infinitude gravitate as a hierarchy round a divine focus? Some day the astronomers of the planets which gravitate in the light of Hercules (towards which constellation the solar system is moving) will see a little star appear in their sky. This will be our sun, carrying us along in its rays; perhaps at this very moment we are visible dust of a sidereal hurricane, in a milky way, the transformer of our destinies. We are mere playthings in the immensity of Infinitude."[†]

It is not strange that men who have learned to look at the universe in this lofty manner should go a step farther, beyond the actually known, and suggest that some of these countless heavenly bodies must be inhabited by living, thinking beings. Sober, thoughtful truthseekers, who never advance needlessly a new theory, have suggested, in all seriousness, that other worlds than ours are peopled. For instance, "What sort of life, spiritual and intellectual, exists in distant worlds? We can not for a moment suppose that our little planet is the only one throughout the whole uni-

Scientists believe that heavenly bodies are inhabited by living, thinking beings.

---

* The Sun, C. A. Young, p. 11.

† Popular Astronomy, C. Flammarion, p. 309.

verse on which may be found the fruits of civilization, warm firesides, friendship, the desire to penetrate the mysteries of creation."*

Such, then, is in very general terms the view of modern astronomy with reference to the constitution of the universe. Most of the information upon which this view rests has been gathered during the last fifty years.

Joseph Smith was doubtlessly impressed with the beauty of the starry heavens, and, in common

Joseph Smith taught that all heavenly bodies are in motion. with all men of poetical nature, allowed his thoughts to wander into the immensity of space. However, he had no known opportunity of studying the principles of astronomy, or of becoming familiar with the astronomical questions that were agitating the thinkers of his day. Naturally, very little is said in his writings that bears upon the planetary and stellar constitution of the universe; yet enough to prove that he was in perfect harmony with the astronomical views developed since his day.

First, he believed that stellar bodies are distributed throughout space. "And worlds without number have I created."† "And there are many kingdoms; for there is no space in which there is no kingdom."‡ He is further in harmony with modern views in that he claims that stars may be destroyed, and new ones formed. "For, behold, there are many worlds that have passed away by the word of my power."‖ "And as one earth shall

---

*The Problems of Astronomy, S. Newcomb.

†Book of Moses, 1: 33.   ‡Doctrine and Covenants, 88: 37.   ‖Book of Moses, 1: 35.

pass away, and the heavens thereof, even so shall another come.''*

At the time that Joseph Smith wrote, there was considerable discussion as to whether the laws of the solar system were effective with the stars. The Prophet had no doubts on that score, for he wrote, ''And unto every kingdom is given a law; and unto every law there are certain bounds also and conditions.''†

Likewise, his opinions concerning the motions of celestial objects were very definite and clear. ''He hath given a law unto all things by which they move in their times and seasons; and their courses are fixed; even the courses of the heavens and the earth, which comprehend the earth and all the planets. The earth rolls upon her wings, and the sun giveth his light by day, and the moon giveth her light by night, and the stars also giveth their light, as they roll upon their wings in glory, in the midst of the power of God.''‡

In another place the same thought is expressed. ''The sun, moon or stars; all the times of their revolutions; all the appointed days, months, and years, and all the days of their days, months, and years, and all their glories, laws, and set times, shall be revealed.''‖

The two revelations from which these quotations are made, were given to the Prophet in 1832 and 1839 respectively, many years before the fact

---

* Doctrine and Covenants, 1: 38.

† Doctrine and Covenants, 88: 38.

‡ Doctrine and Covenants, 88: 43, 45.

‖ Doctrine and Covenants, 121: 30. 31.

that all celestial· bodies are in motion was understood and accepted by the world of science.

The accepted conception that groups or clusters of stars form systems which revolve around
Joseph Smith some one point or powerful star, was
taught that the also clearly understood by Joseph
solar system is Smith, for he speaks of stars of dif-
only one of ferent orders with controlling stars for
many—in ad- each order. "And I saw the stars that
vance of the they were very great, and that one of
astronomers them was nearest unto the throne of God; and there
of his day.
were many great ones which were near unto it: and
the Lord said unto me: These are the governing
ones; and the name of the great one is Kolob because it is near unto me—I have set this one to
govern all those which belong to the same order
as that upon which thou standest."* That the governing star, Kolob, is not the sun is evident, since
the statement is made later in the chapter that the
Lord showed Abraham "Shinehah, which is the
sun." Kolob, therefore, must be a mighty star governing more than the solar system; and is possibly
the central sun around which the ·sun with its attendant planets is revolving. The other great stars
near Kolob are also governing stars, two of which
are mentioned by name Oliblish and Enish-go-on-
dosh, though nothing is said of the order or stars
that they control. The reading of the third chapter
of the *Book of Abraham* leaves complete conviction
that Joseph Smith taught that the celestial bodies
are in great groups, controlled (under gravitational
influence) by large suns. In this doctrine, he anti-

---

* Book of Abraham, chapter 3.

cipated the world of science by many years.

It is perhaps less surprising *to* find that Joseph Smith believed that there are other peopled worlds **Joseph Smith** than ours. For instance, ''The reckon- **taught that** ing of God's time, angel's time, proph- **other worlds are** **inhabited.** et's time, and man's time, is according to the planet on which they reside,''* which distinctly implies that other planets are inhabited. Another passage reads, ''The angels do not reside on a planet like this earth, but they reside in the presence of God, on a globe like a sea of glass and fire.''†

While the idea that the planets and stars may be inhabited is not at all new, yet it is interesting to note that Joseph Smith taught as an absolute truth that such is the case. Probably no other philosopher has gone quite that far.

These brief quotations go to show that the doctrines of the Prophet of the Latter-day Saints are in full accord with the views that distinguish the new astronomy. It is also to be noted that in advancing the theories of universal motion among the stars, and of great stars or suns governing groups of stars, he anticipated by many years the corresponding theories of professional astronomers.

In various sermons the Prophet dealt more fully with the doctrines here set forth and showed more strongly than is done in his doctrinal writings, that he understood perfectly tho far reaching nature of his astronomical teachings.

Did Joseph Smith teach these truths by chance? or, did he receive inspiration from a higher power?

---

* Doctrine and Covenants, 130: 4.

† Loc. cit., verses 6 and 7. See also 88: 61.

Chapter VII.

GEOLOGICAL TIME.

God speaks in various ways to men. The stars, the clouds, the mountains, the grass and the soil, are all, to him who reads aright, forms of divine revelation. Many of the noblest attributes of God may be learned by a study of the laws according to which Omnipotent Will directs the universe.

The history of the world written in the rocks.

Nowhere is this principle more beautifuly illustrated and confirmed than in the rocks that constitute the crust of the earth. On them is written in simple plainness the history of the earth almost from that beginning, when the Spirit of God moved upon the face of the waters. Yet, for centuries, men saw the rocks, their forms and their adaptations to each other, without understanding the message written in them. Only, as the wonderful nineteenth century approached, did the vision open, and the interpretation of the story of the rocks become apparent.

How the earth first came into being has not yet been clearly revealed. From the first, however, the mighty forces which act today, have shaped and fashioned the earth and prepared it for man's habitation. Water, entering the tiny cracks of the rocks, and expanding as, in winter, it changed to ice, crumbled the mighty

Water and heat among the shaping forces of the earth.

mountans; water, falling as rain from the clouds, washed the rock fragments into the low-lying places to form soil; the water in mighty rivers chiseled the earth with irresistible force, as shown by the Grand Canyon of the Colorado. The internal heat of the earth, aided by the translocation of material by water, produced large cracks in the earth's crust, through which oceans of molten matter flowed and spread themselves over the land; the same heat appeared in volcanoes, through which were spurted liquid earth, cinders and foul gases; as the earth heat was lost, the crust cooled, contracted and great folds appeared, recognized as mountains, and as time went on, many of the mountains were caused to sink and the ocean beds were brought up in their stead. Wonderful and mighty have been the changes on the earth's surface since the Lord began its preparation for the race of men.

In the beginning, it appears that water covered the whole earth. In that day, the living creatures **The geological** of earth dwelt in the water, and it was **history of the** the great age of fishes and other aquatic **earth is in many** **chapters.** animals. Soon the first land lifted itself timidly above the surface of the ocean, and formed inviting places for land animals and plants. Upon the land came, first, according to the story of the rocks, a class of animals known as amphibians, like frogs, that could live both in water and on land. Associated with these creatures were vast forests of low orders of plants, that cleared the atmosphere of noxious gases, and made it fit for higher forms of life. Then followed an age in which the predominating animals were gigantic reptiles, a step higher than

the amphibians, but a step lower than the class of
Mammals to which man belongs. During the age of
these prehistoric monsters, the earth was yet more
fully prepared for higher life. Following the age of
reptiles, came the age of mammals, which still persists, though, since the coming of man upon the
earth, the geological age has been known as the age
of man.

This rapid sketch of the geological history of
the earth does very poor justice to one of the most
complete, wonderful and beautiful stories brought to
the knowledge of man. The purpose of this chapter
is not, however, to discuss the past ages of the earth.

It is, of course, readily understood that such
mighty changes as those just described, and the suc-
cession of different kinds of organic life, could not
have taken place in a few years. Vast periods of
time must of necessity have been required for the
initiation, rise, domination and final extinction of
each class of animals. A year is too small a unit of
measurement in geological time; a thousand years or,
better, a million years, would more nearly answer the requirements.

It is possible in various ways to arrive at a conception of the age of the earth since organic life
came upon it. For instance, the gorge
of the Niagara Falls was begun in comparatively recent days, yet, judging by
the rate at which the falls are now receding, it must
have been at least 31,000 years since the making of
the gorge was first begun, and it may have been nearly 400,000 years.* Lord Kelvin, on almost purely

*The earth is
probably mil-
lions of years
old.*

---

* Dana's New Text Book of Geology, p. 375.

physical grounds, has estimated that the earth cannot be more than 100,000,000 years old, but that it
may be near that age.* It need not be said, probably,
that all such calculations are very uncertain, when
the actual number of years are considered; but, all
human knowledge, based upon the present appearance of the earth and the laws that control known
phenomena, agree in indicating that the age of the
earth is very great, running in all probability into
millions of years. It must have been hundreds of
thousands of years since the first life was placed
upon earth.

When these immense periods of time were first
suggested by students of science, a great shout of

**The war con-
cerning the
earth's age has
helped theology
and science.**
opposition arose from the camp of the
theologians. The Bible story of creation had been taken literally, that in
six days did the Lord create the heavens and the earth; and it was held to be blasphemy
to believe anything else. The new revelation, given
by God in the message of the rocks, was reecived as
a man-made theory, that must be crushed to earth.
It must be confessed likewise that many of the men
of science, exulting in the new light, ridiculed the
story told by Moses, and claimed that it was an evidence that the writings of Moses were not inspired,
but merely man-made fables.

The war between the Mosaic and the geological
record of creation became very bitter and lasted long,
and it led to a merciless dissection and scrutiny of
the first chapter of Genesis, as well as of the evidence
upon which rests the geological theory of the age of

---

*Lectures and Addresses, vol. 2, p. 10.

the earth.   When at last the din of the battle grew
faint, and the smoke cleared away, it was quickly per-
ceived by the unbiased on-lookers, that the Bible and
science had both gained by the conflict.   Geology
had firmly established its claim, that the earth was
not made in six days of twenty-four hours each; and
the first chapter of Genesis had been shown to be a
marvelously truthful record of the great events of
creation.

Moses, in the first chapter of Genesis, enumerates
the order of the events of creation.   First, light was
The word day   brought to the earth and was divided
in Genesis   from darkness, "and the evening and
refers to indef-
inite time   the morning were the first day."   Then
periods.   the firmament was established in the
midst of the waters, "and the evening and the morning were the second day."   After each group of
creative events, the same expression occurs, "and
the evening and the morning were the third [fourth,
fifth, and sixth] days."   Those who insisted upon the
literal interpretation of the language of the Bible
maintained that the word day, as used in Genesis 1,
referred to a day of twenty-four hours, and that all
the events of creation were consummated by an all-
powerful God in one hundred and forty-four earthly
hours.   An examination of the original Hebrew for
the use of the word translated "day in Genesis, revealed that it refers more frequently to periods of
time of indefinite duration.*   When this became
clear, and the records of the rocks became better
known, some theologians suggested, that as we are

---

* Compare The Mosaic Record of Creation, A. McCaul,
D. D., p. 213.

told that a thousand years are as one day to God, the day of Genesis 1 refers to periods of a thousand years each. This did not strengthen the argument. The best opinion of today, and it is well-nigh universal, is that the Mosaic record refers to indefinite periods of time corresponding to the great divisions of historical geology.

Even as late as the sixties and seventies of the last century this question was still so unsettled as to warrant the publication of books defending the Mosaic account of creation.*

In 1830, certain visions, given to the Jewish lawgiver Moses, were revealed to the Prophet Joseph

Joseph Smith's teachings concerning creation found in the Book of Abraham. Smith. These visions are now incorporated with other matter in the Pearl of Great Price, under the title, The Book of Moses. In chapter two of this book is found an account of the creation, which is nearly identical with the account found in Genesis 1. The slight variations which occur tend only to make the meaning of the writer clearer. In this account, the expression "and the evening and the morning were the first [etc.] day," occurs just as it does in the Mosaic account in the Bible. In 1835, certain ancient records found in the catacombs of Egypt fell into the hands of Joseph Smith, who found them to be some of the writings of Abraham, while he was in Egypt. The translation of these records is also found in the Pearl of Great Price, under the title, The Book of Abraham. In the fourth and fifth chapters of the book is found an account of the creation

---

* For instance Aids to Faith, containing McCaul's most able discussion. The Origin of the World, J. W. Dawson.

according to the knowledge of Abraham. The two accounts are essentially the same, but the Abrahamic version is so much fuller and clearer that it illumines the obscurer parts of the Mosaic account. We shall concern ourselves here only with the variation in the use of the word " day."

In Genesis 1:5 we read, "And God called the light Day, and the darkness he called Night. And the evening and the morning were the first day." The corresponding period is discussed in the Book of Abraham 4:5 as follows: "And the Gods called the light Day, and the darkness they called Night. And it came to pass that from the evening until the morning they called night; and from the morning until the evening they called day; *and this was the first, or the beginning, of that which they called night and day."*

The Book of Abraham conveys the idea that the creative periods included much time.

It is to be noted that in Abraham's version names were given to the intervals between evening and morning, and morning and evening; but absolutely nothing is said about a *first* day: the statement is simply made, that this was the beginning of the alternating periods of light and darkness which *they,* the Gods, had named night and day. According to this version, the first creative period occupied an unknown period of time.

In Genesis 1:8 it further says: "And God called the firmament Heaven. And the evening and the morning were the second day."

The corresponding passage in the Book of Abraham 4:8, reads, "And the Gods called the expanse Heaven. And it came to pass that it was from evening until morning that they called night; and it came to pass that it was from morning until evening that they called day, and this was *the second time that they called night and day."*

Here it must be noted that nothing is said about a second day. It is said that it was the second time that *they* called day—which leaves the second creative period entirely indefinite so far as time limits are concerned.

In Genesis 1:13, it reads, "and the evening and the morning were the third day."

In Abraham 4:13, the corresponding passage reads, "And it came to pass that they numbered the days; from the evening until the morning they called night; and it came to pass, from the morning until the evening they called day; and it was the third time."

Here it is explicitly stated that the Gods numbered the days; evidently, they counted the days that had passed during the third creative period, and it was the third time that the numbering had been done. Again, the third creative period is left indefinite, as to time limits.

Gen. 1:19, reads, "And the evening and the morning were the fourth day."

Correspondingly, in Abraham 4:19, is found, "And it came to pass that it was from evening until morning that it was night; and it came to pass that it was from morning until evening that it was day; and it was the fourth time."

This quotation from Abraham, standing alone, would be somewhat ambiguous, for it might indicate that it was the fourth time that the periods between evening and morning, and morning and evening were called night and day. In the light of previous passages, however, the meaning of the passage becomes clear. Certainly there is nothing in the verse to confine the fourth creative period within certain time limits.

The fifth day in Genesis closes as does the fourth; and the fifth time in Abraham closes as does the fourth. The remarks made concerning the fourth creative period apply to the fifth.

Concerning the sixth creative period, Gen. 1:31, says, "And God saw everything that he had made, and, behold, it was very good. And the evening and the morning were the sixth day."

Of the same period Abraham says, "And the Gods said: We will do everything that we have said, and organize them; and behold, they shall be very obedient. And it came to pass that it was from morning until evening that they called night; and it came to pass that it was from evening until morning that they called day; and they numbered the sixth time."

As in the previous periods, the sixth ended by the sixth period, like those preceding, being inde- the Gods numbering the days of the creative period; terminate as to time.

Repeated reading and study of the Abrahamic account, as revealed through Joseph Smith, make it certain beyond doubt that the intent is to convey the idea that the creative periods included much time, and that, at the end of each period, the measure of night and day, was applied to the period, in order that its length might be determined. Whether or not the different creative periods represented days to the mighty beings concerned in the creation, we do not know, and it matters little to the argument of this article.*

Now, then, we must remember that Joseph Smith made this translation long before the theologians of the world had consented to admit that the Mosaic days meant long periods of time; and long before geology had established beyond question that immense time periods had been consumed in the preparation of the earth for man.

Joseph Smith, the humble, unlearned, despised boy, unfamiliar with books and the theories of men, stated with clear and simple certainty, if his works be read with the eye of candid truth, this fundamental truth of geological science and the Bible, long before the learned of the world had agreed upon the same truth.†

Standing alone, this fact might be called a chance coincidence, a result of blind fate. But recalling that it is one of many similar and even more

---

* The writer understands the creation, reported in Abraham, 4th chapter, to be spiritual in its nature; but he also believes that this spiritual account is a perfect picture of the actual material creation. If chapter 4 of Abraham represents the Gods planning creation, the measuring of time becomes easily understood. It then means, "How long will it take to accomplish the work?" All this, however, has no bearing upon the present argument.

† It may be remarked that other geological doctrines were taught by the Prophet, that science has since confirmed. One of these was discussed by Dr. J. E. Talmage in the Improvement Era, Vol. 7, p. 481.

striking facts, what shall be said, Has ever impostor dared what Joseph Smith did? Has ever false prophet lived beyond his generation, if his prophecies were examined? Shall we of this foremost age accept convincing, logical truth, though it run counter to our preconceived notions? Glorious were the visions of Joseph the Prophet; unspeakable would be our joy, should they be given to us.

Chapter VIII.

ORGANIZED INTELLIGENCE.

The student of the constitution of the universe must take into account living beings. Plants, animals and men are essentially different from the mass of matter. The rock, apparently, is the same forever; but the plant has a beginning, and after a comparatively short existence dies. Animals and men, likewise, begin their earthly existence; then, after a brief life, die, or disappear from the immediate knowledge of of living things.

A complete philosophy must consider living beings.

Man, the highest type of living things, differs from the rock, moreover, in that he possesses the power to exercise his will in directing natural forces. Animals and even plants seem to possess a similar power to a smaller degree. The rock on the hillside is pulled downward by gravitation, but can move only if the ground is removed from beneath it by some external force. Man, on the other hand, can walk up or down the hill, with or against the pull of gravity.

Modern science refers all phenomena to matter and motion; in other words, to matter and force or energy. In this general sense, matter includes the universal ether, and force includes any or all of the forces known, or that may be known, to man.

Science teaches that all phenomena may be referred to matter and ether in motion.

To illustrate: the electrician develops a current

of electricity, which to the scientist is a portion of the universal ether moving in a certain definite manner. When the vibrations of the ether are caused to change, light, or magnetism or chemical affinity may result from the electricity. In every case, matter is in motion. The ear perceives a certain sound. It is produced by the movements of the air. In fact, sounds are carried from place to place by great air waves. The heat of the stove is due to the rapid vibration of the molecules in the iron of the stove, which set up corresponding vibrations in the ether.

In nature no exceptions have been found to the great scientific claim that all natural phenomena may be explained by referring them to matter in motion. *Variations in the kind of matter and the kind of motion, lead to all the variations found in the universe.

By many it has been held that life and its phenomena transcend the ordinary explanations of nature. Yet, those who have learned, by laborious researches, that the fundamental ideas of **Life is a certain form of motion.** the universe are only eternal matter, eternal energy and the universe-filling medium, the ether, find it very difficult to conceive of a special force of life, which concerns itself solely with very limited portions of matter, and is wholly distinct from all other natural forces.

To the student of science it seems more consistent to believe that life is nothing more than matter in motion; that, therefore, all matter possesses a kind of life; and that the special life possessed by plants, animals and man, is only the highest or most com-

---

* Tyndall, Fragments of Science, I. chaps. I and II.

plex motion in the universe. The life of man, according to this view, is essentially different from the life of the rock; yet both are certain forms of the motion of matter, and may be explained ultimately by the same fundamental conceptions of science. Certainly, such an idea is more beautifully simple than that of a special force of life, distinct from all other natural forces.

It is argued by those who uphold this view, that the simple forces of nature are converted by living things into the higher forces that characterize life. For instance, to keep the human body, with its wonderful will and intelligence, in health, it is necessary to feed it. The food is actually burned within the body. The heat thus obtained gives to the man both physical and intellectual vigor. It would really appear, therefore, that heat, which is a well known, simple physical force, may be converted by the animal body into other and more complex forces, or modes of motion, such as the so-called life force.

Naturally, should science class life as the highest or most complex of the modes of material motion, **A certain** the question would arise concerning the **organization char-**manner in which this conversion were **acterizes life.** made possible. The answer must be that the ultimate particles of the matter composing the living thing are so arranged or organized that the great natural forces may be converted into life force. It is possible by passing heat through certain substances to make them luminous, thus converting heat into light; by employing a dynamo, mechanical energy may be converted into electrical energy; by coiling a wire around a rod of soft iron, electricity may be converted into magnetism.   In short, it is well understood in science, that by the use of the right machines one form of energy may be changed into another.   It is generally assumed, that the human body is so organized that the forces of heat, light and undoubtedly others, may be converted into higher forms, peculiar to living things.*

To substantiate this view, it may be recalled that the fundamental chemical individual in living
Protoplasm, a highly organized body, is always associated with life. thing is a very complex, unstable substance known as protoplasm. No living cell exists without the presence of this substance. It is far from being known well, as yet, but enough is known to enable science to say that it is composed of several elements, so grouped and regrouped as to transcend all present methods of research.† By means of this highly organized body, it is assumed that the ordinary forces of nature are worked over and made suited for the needs of the phenomena of life.

The existence of the complex life-characteristic substance protoplasm, renders probable the view that living things, after all, differ from the rest of creation only in the kind and degre of their organization, and that life, as the word is ordinarily used, depends upon a certain kind or organization of matter,‡ which leads to a certain kind of motion.

As to the origin of the special organization

---

* Compare, Fiske, Outlines of Cosmic Philiosophy, chap. XVI.   Pearson, Grammar of Science, pp. 404-407.   Dolbear, Matter, Ether and Motion, chap. XI, pp. 294-297.

† Pearson, Grammar of Science, p. 408.

‡ Tyndall, Fragments of Science. II, chaps. IV and VI.

called life, science has nothing to say. Science is helpless when she deals with the beginning of things. The best scientific explanation of life is that it is a very complex mode of motion occasioned by a highly complex organization of the matter and ether of the living body.

There are still some students who prefer to believe in the existence of a special vital force, which is not subject to the laws that govern other forces. This view, however, is so inconsistent with the modern understanding of the contents of the universe that it has few followers.

The view that life is a special organization by which the great natural forces are focussed and concentrated, so as to accomplish the **The modern conception of life is very recent.** greatest works, necessarily implies a belief in the modern laws of nature. Since modern science is of very recent development it was quite improbable for such a conception of life to have been held clearly before modern times. In fact it is within the last thirty or forty years that these views have found expression among scientific investigations.

As observed in chapters two and three, Joseph Smith taught that the energy of matter or of ether **Joseph Smith taught the universality of life.** is a form of intelligence. If, according to this doctrine, matter and ether are intelligent; then life also must reside in all matter and ether. eHnce everything in the universe is alive. Further, since all force is motion, universal motion is universal life. The difference between rock, plant, beast and man is in the amount and organization of its life or intelligence. For instance, in harmony with this doctrine, the earth must possess intelligence or life. In fact the Prophet says "the earth......shall be sanctified; yea, notwithstanding it shall die, it shall be quickened again, and shall abide the power by which it is quickened."* The statement that the earth shall die and shall be quickened again, certainly implies that the earth possess life, though, naturally, of an order wholly different from that of men or other higher living things.

It is an established "Mormon" doctrine that man is coexistent with God. Note the following state-

Man is coexistent with God.
ments: "Ye were also in the beginning with the Father." "Man was also in the beginning with God. Intelligence, or the light of truth, was not created or made, neither indeed can be."† "Yet these two spirits, notwithstanding one is more intelligent than the other, have no beginning; they existed before, they shall have no end, they shall exist after for they are eternal."‡

In the account of the Creation, given in the Book of Abraham, it is clearly stated that the Gods or-

Joseph Smith taught that man is organized from matter, spirit and Intelligence
ganized the earth and all upon it from available materials, and as the fitting climax to their labors they "went down to organize man in their own image, in the image of Gods to form him."§ The creation of man was in part at least the organization of individuals from eternal materials and forces. The nature of that organization is made partly clear by the

---

* Doctrine and Covenants 88: 25, 26.

† Doctrine and Covenants 93: 23 and 29.

‡ Book of Abraham 3: 19.

§ Book of Abraham, 4th chap. (Note verse 27.)

Prophet when he says "The spirit and the body are the soul of man."* The spirit here referred to may be compared to the ether of science, vibrating with the force of intelligence, which is the first and highest of the many forces of nature. The body, similarly, refers to the grosser elements, also fired with the universal energy—intelligence. The word *Soul,* in the above quotation, means man as he is on earth and is used as in Genesis. Man, according to this, is composed of matter; the spirit which may be likened to ether, and energy. The organization of man at the begininng of our earth history, was only the clothing of the eternal spiritual man with the matter which constitutes the perishable body. In confirmation of this view note another statement, "For man is spirit. The elements are eternal, and spirit and element, inseparably connected, receiveth a fullness of joy, and when separated, man can not receive a fullness of joy."† Here also it is taught that man is composed of matter, spirit and energy.

President Brigham Young has left an interesting paragraph that confirms the statement that according to "Mormon" doctrine, all matter is intelligent, and that man is superior only because of his higher organization. "Is this earth, the air and the water, composed of life......? ......If the earth, air and water, are composed of life is there any intelligence in this life?....Are those particles of matter life; if so, are they in possession of intelligence according to the grade of their organization?......We suggest

Intelligence is universal.

---

* Doctrine and Covenants 88: 15.

† Doctrine and Covenants 93: 33 and 34.

the idea that there is an eternity of life, an eternity of organization, and an eternity of intelligence from the highest to the lowest grade, every creature in its order, from the Gods to the animalculae.''*

The statement that man can receive a fullness of joy only when spirit and element are united, is of it-

Spirit unaided knows matter with difficulty. self a scientific doctrine of high import. This is a world of matter; and a spiritual man, that is, one made only of the universal ether, would not be able to receive fully the impressions that come from the contact of element with element. To enjoy and understand this world, it is necessary for the spirit to be clothed with matter. The ether or spirit world is not within our immediate view; and it is probable that the material world is far away from purely spiritual beings.

This whole doctrine means that God is the organizer of worlds, and all upon them. He is not the

God is the Master-builder. Creator of the materials and forces of the universe, for they are eternal; He is the master builder who uses the simple elements of nature for his purposes. It is also plain that, according to ''Mormon'' doctrine, there is no special life force. The intelligence residing in a stone is in quality, as far as it goes, the same as the intelligence possessed by man. But, man is so organized that a greater amount of intelligence, a fullness of it, centers in him, and he is as a consequence essentially and eternally different from the stone. President Young also said, ''The life that is within us is a part of an eternity of life, and is organized spirit, which is clothed upon by tabernacles, thereby

---

* The Resurrection, p. 3. Ed. of 1884.

constituting our present being, which is designed for the attainment of further intelligence. The matter comprising our bodies and spirits has been organized from the eternity of matter that fills immensity,"*

This doctrine does not permit of the interpretation that a lower intelligence, such as that of an animal, may in time become the intelligence of a man. "It remaineth in the sphere in which I, God, created it."† The horse will ever remain a horse, though the intelligence of the animal may increase. To make any of the constituent parts or forces of an animal, part of the intelligence of a man, it would be necessary to disorganize the animal; to organize the elements into a man, and thus to begin over again.

A lower intelligence can not become a higher intelligence except by disorganization.

Men, beasts and plants—those beings that possess the higher life, differ from inanimate nature, so called, by a higher degree of organization. That is the dogma of "Mormonism," and the doctrine of science. About 1831 Joseph Smith gave this knowledge to the world; a generation later, scientfic men arrived independently at the same conclusion.

Joseph Smith anticipated science in the modern conception of life.

The thinkers and writers of "Mormonism" have more or less directly taught the same doctrine. Apostle Orson Pratt believed that the body of man, both spiritual and earthly, was composed of atoms or ultimate particles—of the Holy Spirit for the spiritual body and material elements for the mortal body. It has already been shown that

The thinkers and writers of Mormonism have taught the foregoing doctrine of life.

---

* Journal of Discourses, vol. 7: 285. (Brigham Young.)

† Book of Moses 3: 9.

the Holy Spirit of "Mormonism" may be compared with the ether of science, vibrating with the greater force of the universe—intelligence.   For instance: "The intelligent particles of a man's spirit are by their peculiar union, but one human spirit."* "Several of the atoms of this spirit exist united to-gether in the form of a person."† Undoubtedly Elder Pratt believed that the living man is simply organized from the elements and elementary forces of the universe.

Perhaps the best and safest exposition of the philosophy of "Mormonism" is Parley P. Pratt's Key to Theology. In it he states definitely that the spirit of man is organized from the elementary Holy Spirit. "The holiest of all elements, the Holy Spirit, when organized in individual form, and clothed upon with flesh and bones, contains, etc."‡   That the earthly body was likewise organized is equally plain for he says "At the commencement—the elements—were found in a state of chaos."§   Then man was "moulded from the earth as a brick."** Again, "The spirit of man consists of an organization of the elements of spiritual matter,"†† which finds entrance into its tabernacle of flesh. In another place he defines creation by asking "What is creation? Merely organization.......The material of which this earth was made always did exist, and it was only an or-

---

* Absurdities of Immaterialism, ed. 1849, p. 26.

† Ibid, p. 29.

‡ Key to Theology, 5h ed., p. 46.

§ Ibid, p. 49

** Ibid, p. 51.

†† Ibid, p. 131.

ganization which took place during the time spoken of by Moses."*

Numerous other authorities might be quoted to prove that the above is the "Mormon" view.†

In this chapter the intention has not been to explain fully the doctrines of Joseph Smith relating to the nature of man, but to call attention to the fact that the present scientific conception of the nature of living things is the same as that of "Mormonism." That "Mormonism" goes farther than science, and completes the explanation, is to the credit of the Prophet.

It must not be forgotten that in stating the doctrine that man is organized from the eternal elements and elementary forces of the universe, in such a way as to produce the phenomena of higher life, Joseph Smith anticipated the workers in science by nearly a generation.

How wonderful was this boy-prophet of "Mormonism," if all this was orginated within his own mind! At every point of contact, the sanest of modern philosophy finds counterpart in the theological structure of the Gospel as taught by Joseph Smith. Is the work divine?

---

* Roberts, Mormon Doctrine of Diety, pp. 278, 279.

† See especially the Prophet Joseph Smith's Sermon, Contributor, vol. 4, pp. 256-268.

Chapter IX.

FAITH.

For the government of the individual the first principle in Mormon theology is faith. Joseph Smith defined faith in the words of the Apostle Paul, "Now, faith is the substance of things hoped for; the evidence of things not seen." To this the Prophet added "From this we learn that faith is the assurance which men have of things which they have not seen."* On this principle, with this definition, many young persons who have ventured upon the sea of unbelief have wrecked the religion of their childhood; for, the human mind, in some stages of its development, is disinclined to accept as knowledge anything that can not be sensed directly.

Faith is the assurance of the existence of "things not seen."

Nowadays, the young doubter who can not accept as the foundation of his religion "things which he has not seen," usually turns for comfort and future growth to the results of science. There he finds truths upon truths, glorious in their beauty and susceptibility to direct and unmistakeable proof; and soon he declares that in so-called natural science, there is no need of faith, for, if a person has only advanced far enough, every concern of science may be known through one, two or several senses.

* Doctrine and Covenants, Lecture I, verses 8, 9.

It is true that in the beginning of science no faith seems to be required; for every statement is based on experiments and observations that may be repeated by every student; and nothing is "taken on trust." As the deeper parts of science are explored, however, it is soon discovered that in science as in theology, a faith in "things that can not be seen," is an essential requisite for progress. In fact, the fundamental laws of the great divisions of science deal with realities that are wholly and hopelessly beyond the reach of man's five senses.

Such faith lies at the formation of science.

An exposition of the fundamental conception of chemical science will illustrate the nature of scientific faith. A fragment of almost any substance may easily be divided into two or three pieces by a stroke of a hammer. Each of the pieces may be broken into smaller pieces and this process of division continued until the powder is as fine as dust. Still, each particle of the dust may be divided again and again, if we only have instruments fine enough to continue the process. A question which philosophy asked itself near its beginning was: Is it possible to keep on dividing the dust particles forever, or is there a particle so small that it can not be divided again? Neither science nor abstract philosophy has yet been able to answer this question fully. However, science has learned that if such a process of division occurs, in course of time a particle will be obtained which is so small that if it is divided or broken, the fragments will no longer be of the same nature as the original substance. These smallest par-

The molecules are beyond man's direct senses.

ticles in which the properties of the orignal substance inhere, are known as *molecules.* Thus a molecule of sugar, when broken, falls into the elements carbon, hydrogen and oxygen; of salt, into sodium and chlorine and of water into hydrogen and oxygen.

The size of such a molecule can not be comprehended by the human mind; its smallness seems infinite. The mortal eye, though aided by the most powerful miscroscopes of modern days could not distinguish a sugar molecule or even a pile of thousands of them; placed on the tongue, there would be no sensation of sweetness; though it were hurled against our body with the velocity of lightning we should not feel the impact. To all our senses, the molecule is wholly unknown and no doubt shall remain so while the earth is as it is. Yet, no fact is better established than the existence of the realities that we interpret as molecules. Their relative weights and other properties have been securely determined. The existence of such a particle is as certain as is the existence of the sun in the high heavens.

Not only does science teach the existence of molecules; it looks within them and reveals their composition. For instance, a molecule of the sugar known as glucose, and used by candy makers, is made up of six particles of the element carbon, twelve of the element hydrogen and six of the element oxygen. The particles of carbon in the glucose molecule are so small that if one were divided it would no longer be carbon; the same with the particles of hydrogen and oxygen: if divided they would change into some-

Science teaches the composition of the directly unknowable molecules.

thing else—into what is not yet known to man. These smallest particles are called *atoms* of the elements charcoal, hydrogen and oxygen. If instead of an atom of carbon, hydrogen and oxygen, we write C, H, O, the composition of a molecule of glucose would be written $C_6H_{12}O_6$ These are also indisputable facts of science. If the molecules are far beyond the range of our senses, the atoms are of course much further removed from the known world.

But the chemist does not stop here. He is able to state accurately how the invisible, unsensed atoms **Science teaches** are arranged within the unknowable **the arrange-** molecule. In nature are found several **ments of the** **atoms within the** glucose-like sugars, the molecules of **molecules.** which contain the same numbers of carbon, hydrogen and oxygen atoms. The varying properties of these sugars have been found to result from the different arrangements of the atoms within the molecules. The structure of the molecules of three of the most common sugars are as follows:

I DEXTROSE *	II LAEVULOSE *	III GALACTOSE *
H_2=C—OH	H^2=C—O H	H^2=C—OH
HO--C—H	H O—C—H	HO-C H
HO--C—H	H O—C—H	HC—OH
H—C—O-H	H C—O H	HC—OH
HO--C—H	C=O	HO-CH
H—C=O	H C=O	H—C=O

* Dextrose and laevulose combine to form ordinary cane or beet sugar. Dextrose and galactose combine to form the sugar found in milk.

Referring to the above diagrams it will be observed that although each arrangement contains the same number of atoms, yet, because of the difference in arrangement, they are far from being identical. In fact, the difference in the properties of the sugars may be referred to the arrangement of the atoms in the molecules. This truth is one of the most splendid achievements of modern science. All the facts, here briefly outlined, are included in the atomic hypothesis, which is the foundation of the modern science of chemistry.

Science asks us to believe in the existence of particles, unknowable to our senses, the molecules; **Science requires a strong faith in "things not seen."** then to believe in still smaller particles, the atoms, which make up the molecules but whose relative weights and general properties have been determined. Here, a faith is required in "things that can not be seen," and in the properties of these things. True, the scientist does not pretend to describe the atoms in detail, he does not need to do that to establish the certainty of their existence. He looks upon them as ultimate causes of effects that he may note with his physical senses. Does theology require more? Does any sane man in asking us to believe in God, for instance, attempt to describe him in detail?

The scientist goes farther than this, however, for he asks us not only to have faith in the invisible, untasteable, unfeelable atoms, but also in the exact manner in which these atoms are arranged within the molecule. True, it is claimed, only, that the relative arrangement is known, yet the faith required still leads us far beyond the simple faith in atoms. Has any man asked us to believe that he can describe the structure of God's dwelling? No principle taught by Joseph Smith requires a larger faith than this.

Not only in chemistry are such transcendant truths required. The fundamental conception of **The conception** physics requires, if possible, a larger **of the ether re-** faith. The explanations of modern **quires large** **faith.** physics rest largely upon the doctrine of the universal ether. This ether is everywhere present, between the molecules and atoms; in fact the things of the universe are, as it were, suspended in the ocean of ether. This ether is so attenuated that it fills the pores of the human body without impressing itself upon our consciousness, yet some of its properties indicate that its elasticity is equal to that of steel. As shown in chapter 5, the most eminent scientists of the day declare that the existence of this world-ether is one of the few things of which men may be absolutely sure. Yet the ether cannot be seen, heard, tasted, smelled or felt. To our senses it has neither weight nor substance. To believe the existence of this ether requires a faith which is certainly as great as the greatest faith required by Mormon theology.

Numerous other illustrations might be cited, without greatly emphasizing the truth that the great fundamental doctrines of science require a great faith in realities that are beyond the reach of our senses.

The great foundations of science have not come as a "great wakening light," but have come

Faith comes slowly and naturally.

slowly, through a process of normal, guided growth. The first experiment was made, from which a simple conclusion was drawn; the second experiment furnished a second conclusion; the two results combined produced a third conclusion, and so on through thousands of experiments and conclusions, until the brilliant conceptions of modern science were attained. In short, the scientist works very simply by careful observation of nature, "the earth and its fullness," and by as careful reasoning from the observed facts. The mind builds noble structures of the materials the senses bring. The same method may be employed in gaining faith in the principles of theology; and the Apostle Paul tells us distinctly that the righteousness of God is revealed from "faith to faith," and that the eternal power of God and the Godhead and "the invisible things of Him from the creation of the world are clearly seen, being understood by the things that are made." The scientist, likewise, begins with the things that are made and proceeds "from faith to faith," gaining "here a little, and there a little," until a faith is reached which, to him who has not followed its growth, may seem absurd in its loftiness.

Certainly, no man can progress in science unless he has faith in the great inductions of scientific men.

Science cannot progress without faith.

Faith is as indispensable for scientific progress as for theological advancement. In both cases it is the great principle of action.

This subject merits more extended discussion, but the exposition of the nature of faith is outside the argument running through these chapters. It must be sufficient to remark again that Mormonism is strictly scientific in stating as the first principle of the guidance of the individual, that of faith in unseen things; for that is the basic principle for the beginner in modern science.*

* Read for a fuller exposition, We walk by Faith, Improvement Era, Volume 3, p. 561.

Chapter X.

REPENTANCE.

The second principle for the government of the individual, according to Mormon theology, is repentance. So commonly has this principle been discussed from its relation to moral law that its counterpart in all human effort has often been overlooked.

To repent is first to turn from old practices. Thus, he who violates any of God's laws renders

Repentance follows faith. himself liable to certain punishment, but, if he repents, and sins no more, the punishments are averted. Naturally, such a change of heart and action can come only after faith has been established. No man will change a habit without a satisfactory reason. In fact, all the actions of men should be guided by reason. Repentance then is a kind of obedience or active faith; and is great in proportion to the degree of faith posesed by the individual. Certainly, the repentance of no man can transcend his faith, which includes his knowledge.

So it is in science. For centuries, wounds of the body were treated according to certain methods,

Scientific repentance follows scientific faith. assumed to be correct; and, especially in time of war, large numbers of the patients died. Then it was found that low forms of life—the bacteria—infected the wounds, and caused the high mortality. This led to the antiseptic treatment in surgery, which destroys germ life, and leaves the wound absolutely clean. As a consequence the mortality from flesh and other wounds has diminished remarkably. The medical profession repented, or turned away, from its former methods, and the reward was immediately felt. However, before antisceptic surgery was finally and fully established, faith in the practice had to be awakened among the members of the profession. A chemist, making refined analysis may apply a certain factor, assumed to be correct in his calculations, but in reality incorrect. As a result, the determinations are wrong. When later, the correct factor is discovered, and applied, the results of the work become correct. Repentance from the previous error, changes the chemist's work from wrong to right. In fact, in any department of knowledge, when it is discovered that a law of nature has been violated, it becomes necessary, if further progress is desired, to cease the violation. Should a scientist persist in violation of a known law, he knows that the consequences, great or small will certainly follow.

To repent is more than to turn from incorrect practices. It implies also the adoption of new habits. The man who has turned from his sins, may learn of a law, which he has never violated, yet which if obeyed, means progress for him. If he does not follow such a law, but remains neutral in its presence, he certainly is a sinner. To repent from such sin, is to obey each higher law as it appears. In the spiritual life, it is impossible for the person who desires the greatest joy to remain passive in the presence of new principles. He must embrace them; live them; make them his own.

Repentance means adopting new habits; not simply turning from old ones.

Not only must the worker in science turn from

scientific error; he must also accept new science as it is discovered. When the chemist, working with the best known analytical methods, learns that a more rapid or more accurate method has been found, he must adopt the new fact, in order to make the results of his work more accurate. When the chemists of a hundred years ago learned of the atomic hypothesis, it became necessary to adopt it, in order to insure more rapid progress in chemistry. Those who failed to accept the new doctrine worked in greater darkness, and made no material progress. Newton's doctrine of gravitation opened a new method of investigating the universe. Those who did not adopt it were soon outdistanced by their more active colleagues.

In every such case, the obedience yielded to the new knowledge is a kind of repentance. When a person, in religion or science, ceases to break law, he ceases from active evil; when he accepts a new law, he ceases from passive evil. No repentance can be complete which does not cease from both active and passive evil.

Viewed in this manner, then, repentance is obedience to law and is active faith. The law, be-
Repentance is active faith. fore it is obeyed, must be understood—that is, faith must precede repentance. Therefore, the obedience yielded can increase only with the knowledge or faith of the individual. As the Prophet Joseph Smith stated it, "No man can be saved in ignorance" and "a person is saved no faster than he gains intelligence."

Repentance is as truly the second principle of action for individuals, in the domain of science as of theology.

Chapter XI.

BAPTISM.

A repentant man turns from previous violation of law, and accepts every new law that may be revealed to him. Repentance is obedience; and the repentant person is always ready to obey righteous laws.

Baptism is one of the laws of the Kingdom of God. "Except ye repent and be baptized ye can in nowise enter the Kingdom of God." The repentant person must of necessity accept this law with the others with which he may be familiar.

Students of science, who agree that faith and repentance have a place in science, frequently assert **The equivalent of baptism found in science.** that the equivalent of baptism is not found in external nature. This claim may be proved false by examining the nature of law.

The chemist must frequently produce the gas hydrogen. To do it, an acid must be poured upon fragments of certain metals. In thus producing the gas, the chemist obeys law. The astronomer who studies the stars discovers that by using a piece of glass properly ground, his powers of vision appear to be strengthened. He therefore prepares such lenses for his telescopes, and thus obeys law. The surgeon uses antsiceptics in the treatment of wounds because he has learned that such application will destroy germ life, and thus the surgeon obeys law.

The electrician has found that by winding a wire in a certain manner around iron and rotating it near a magnet, electric currents are set up. He builds dynamos according to such principles, and thus shows his obedience to law.

It must be noted that the scientist does not know just *why* acid added to metal produces hydrogen, or *why* a certain curved lens brings the stars nearer; or *why* certain chemicals destroy low forms of life or *why* wire wound in a certain way when rotated in the magnetic field will produce electricity. Nature requires, without volunteering an explanation, that to produce hydrogen, see the stars, destroy germs and produce the electric current, certain invariable laws must be obeyed.

Baptism is essentially of the same nature. To enter the Kingdom of God, a person must be baptized. Just *why* baptism should be the ordinance that opens the door, no man knows. It undoubtedly has high symbolic value; but the symbolism might be expressed in many other ways. All that man can do is to obey.

Men say at times that they will do nothing which they do not fully understand, and therefore they will not be be baptized. It would be **It is unreasonable to do only what is fully understood.** as unreasonable for a man to say that because he does not fully understand why a certain winding of the wire is neccessary to produce electricity he will not produce this wonderful natural force. All theology and all science contain laws that must be obeyed in order to obtain certain results, although the full reasons for the required combinations are not understood.

He who is baptized, enters the Kingdom of God.

He who throws acid on metal enters the kingdom of hydrogen; he who grinds the lens right, enters the kingdom of the stars; he who uses antisceptics right, enters the kingdom of lower life, and he who winds the wire correctly, enters the kingdom of electricity. Yielding obedience to any of these various laws, is a form of baptism, which gives entrance to a kingdom.

The essential virtue of baptism is obedience to law. The prime value of any natural law is at-

Baptism is obedience to law. tained only after obedience has been yielded to it. Baptism is conformity to certain details in entering God's Kingdom. Scientific baptism is conformity to certain details in entering the kingdom of science. Only by baptism can a man attain salvation; only by using lenses of the right curvature can a man view the stars. Religious success does not rest in the degree to which every law is explained; but rather in the degree to which all known laws are obeyed. Scientific success does not rest upon the degree to which every law is explained; but rather in the degree to which every discovered law is obeyed and applied for man's advancement.

In science and in theology man must be content "to see through a glass, darkly." Until the essential nature of infinitude itself shall be understood, man must be content to learn to use unexplained laws. Science is the great explainer, but she explains relations and not the absolute foundations of phenomena.

After faith or knowledge has been obtained, the alpha and omega of religious or scientific progress

is obedience.   The cry of universal nature is, Obedience!

Viewed rationally, therefore, the baptism taught in theology is an ordinance which has its counterpart in every department of science. Joseph Smith was strcitly scientific in classing baptism as the third great principle governing human action.

Chapter XII.

THE GIFT OF THE HOLY GHOST.

Baptism by water is insufficient to open the door to God's Kingdom. The Gift of the Holy Ghost, obtained by the laying on of Hands by one having authority, completes the ordinance. Not only Joseph Smith, but the Savior Himself taught distinctly that to enter the Kingdom of God, a person must be baptized by water and by fire; and the promise is given that those are "baptized by water for the remission of sins, shall receive the Holy Ghost."*

The gift of the Holy Ghost is a gift of intelligence.

Jesus, speaking to His disciples, taught that "the Comforter, which is the Holy Ghost, whom the Father will send in my name, He shall teach you all things, and bring all things to your remembrance, whatsoever I have said unto you."† This clearly implies that the promised gift is essentially a gift of increased intelligence with the added power that results from a more intelligent action. That this is the Mormon view of of the effect of the Gift of the Holy Ghost may be amply demonstrated from the standard works of the Church and from the writings of the leading interpreters of Mormon doctrine. Parley P. Pratt in the Key to Theology says, "It quickens all the intellectual faculties, increases, enlarges, expands and purifies all the natural pas-

---

* Doctrine and Covenants, 84: 63, 64.

† John 14: 26.

sions and affection * * * *. It develops and in-
vigorates all the faculties of the physical and intellectual man.''* The Prophet Joseph Smith declared ''This first Comforter or Holy Ghost has no
other effect than pure intelligence. It is * * * *
powerful in expanding the mind, enlightening the
understanding, and storing the intellect with present
knowledge.''† Concisely expressed, therefore,
Joseph Smith and the Church he restored, teach
that the Gift of the Holy Ghost, is a gift of ''intelligence.''

If the equivalents of faith, repentance and baptism are irrevocable laws for the individual who
Science furnishes studies science, the question arises, Is
an equivalent there also, a scientific equivalent for
of the gift of
the Holy Ghost. the Gift of the Holy Ghost? Even a
superficial view of the matter will reveal such an
equivalent. To use again the illustrations employed
in the preceding chapter, if the chemist has obeyed
natural law in producing hydrogen, that is, has
been baptized into the kingdom of hydrogen, he may
by the proper use and study of the gas obtained,
add much to his knowledge. He may learn that it
is extremely light; that it forms an explosive mix-
ture with air; that it will destroy many vegetable
colors, and will burn with an almost invisible flame.
Thus, the possession of the gas enlarges the knowledge and develops the intelligence of the scientist.
Is not this another form of the Gift of the Holy
Ghost?

The man who is baptized into the kingdom of

* Key to Theology, 5th ed., pp. 101, 102.

† History of the Church, Vol. III, p. 380.

heavenly bodies by grinding the lenses right, is enabled to learn many new facts concerning the nature and motions of celestial bodies; and thus receives intelligence. He who obediently winds the wire correctly around the iron core, may generate a current of electricity with which many mighty works may be accomplished. Do not these men, as their intelligences are expanded, receive a Gift of the Holy Ghost, as a reward for their obedience to the demands of nature?

It would be possible to carry the comparisons into every scientific action without strengthening the argument. In science, if a person has faith, repentance and is baptized, that is obeys, he will receive added intelligence, which is the equivalent of the Gift of the Holy Ghost as taught in theology. The four fundamental laws for the guidance of the individual are identical in Mormon theology, and in modern science.

Just why the laying on of hands should be necessary to complete the ordinance of baptism is not known, any more than the reasons are known for the results that follow the numberless relations that may be established by mortal man. However, the dogma of the Gift of the Holy Ghost, is logically the fourth step in attaining scientific salvation.

Thus, each of the minor laws of Mormonsim might be investigated, and be shown to have a scientific counterpart. For the purpose of this volume, however, a more extended consideration of the laws governing the actions of the individual, is unnecessary.

Chapter XIII.

THE WORD OF WISDOM.

It has already been remarked that the nature of the mission of Joseph Smith made it unlikely that references to scientific matters, and much less to isolated scientific facts, obtainable by proper methods of experimentation should be found in the writings of the Prophet. Nevertheless, in a revelation given March 8, 1883, statements are made that can now be connected with facts of science, not generally or not at all known, at the time the revelation was received.

The doctrine that alcohol is injurious to man is scientific. "Inasmuch as any man drinketh wine or strong drink among you, it is not good, * * * strong drinks are not for the belly but for the washing of your bodies."*

At the time this was written, many persons believed that the use of alcoholic drinks was injurious to human health; but more, especially among the uneducated classes, held quite the opposite opinion. Since that day, the question concerning the value of alcohol in any form has been greatly agitated, and much new light has been obtained. This is not the place to examine this famous controversy, but a few quotations from authoritative books, which are not controversial in their nature, will show the coincidence between the position of science, and the doctrine of Joseph Smith, in respect to this matter.

* Doctrine and Covenants, 89: 5, 7.

The *United States Dispensatory* (17th ed.) speaks of the medicinal properties of alcohol as follows, "It is irritant even to the skin, and much more so to the delicate organs; hence, the various abdominal inflammations that are so frequent in habitual drunkards. A single dose of it, if large enough, may produce death. The nervous symptoms caused by alcohol show that it has a very powerful and direct influence upon the nerve-centers. The arterial pressure and the pulse-rate are both increased by moderate doses of alcohol, by a direct influence upon the heart itself. * * * Taken habitually in excess, alcohol produces the most deplorable results, and is a very common cause of fatal maladies."*

Dr. W. Gilman Thompson in his authoritative book on *Practical Dietetics,* speaking of the constant use of alcoholic beverages, says, "The use of alcohol in any shape is wholly unnecessary for the use of the human organism in health. * * * * The life-long use of alcohol in moderation does not necessarily shorten life or induce disease in some persons, while in others it undoubtedly produces gradual and permanent changes which tend to weaken vital organs so that the resistance of the body to disease is materially impaired. * * * * Many persons should be particularly warned against the use of alcohol. * * * * Although alcohol is such a strong force-producer and heat-generator, its effect in this direction is very soon counter-balanced by its stronger influence in lowering the general tone of the nervous system and in producing positive degeneration in the tissues."*

---

* Page 129, art., Alcohol Ethylicum.   * Pages 206, 207.

The recent newspaper statements that alcohol has been shown to be a food are based on a complete misunderstanding. The experiments demonstrated that alcohol is burned within the body—which is the simplest manner in which the body can rid itself of the alcohol.

No more authoritative opinions on this subject can be found than those contained in the two volumes from which quotations have been made—and the strongest opinions are not quoted. In spite of the isolated claims made for alcohol, the fact remains that the knowledge of the world indicates that alcohol is a poison to the human system; that it is not "for the belly." However, the value of the external use of alcohol, for various purposes, has never been denied. On the contrary almost every up to date practitioner recommends the external use of alcohol, as for instance after baths for lowering the temperature of fever patients. In this matter, then, Joseph Smith was in perfect harmony with the latest results of science. It is strange that he, unlearned as he was, should have stated what is now known as truth, so clearly and simply, yet so emphatically, more than seventy years ago, before the main experiments on the effect of alcohol on the human organsim had been made.

"And again, tobacco is not for the body, neither for the belly, and is not good for man, but is an

The doctrine that tobacco is injurious to man is scientific. herb for bruises and all sick cattle, to Be used with judgment and skill."* Although tobacco has been used for several centuries by civilized man, the real cause of the ef-

* Doctrine and Covenants, 89: 8.

fect which it has upon the human body was not understood until the early part of the last century. In 1809, a chemist separated from tobacco an active principle, in an impure state, some of the properties of which he observed. In 1822, two other chemists succeeded in isolating the same principle, in a pure condition, and found it to be a colorless, oily liquid, of which two to eight per cent is found in all tobacco. This substance has been called nicotine; later investigations have shown it to be one of the most active poisons known. Tobacco owes its activity entirely to this poison."[*]

The intensely poisonous nature of nicotine is illustrated by a number of cases on record. One drop placed on the tongue of a cat caused immediate prostration, and death in seventy-eight seconds. A smaller drop was placed on the tongue of another cat, which resulted in death after two minutes and a half. A third cat to which a similar quantity had been administered was dead after seventy-five seconds. A man who was accustomed to smoking took a chew of tobacco, and after a quarter of an hour accidently swallowed the mass. An hour later he became unconscious and died. In another case, in which an ounce of tobacco had been swallowed, death resulted in seven hours. In still another case, one ounce of tobacco was boiled in water, and the solution drunk as an remedy for constipation. The patient died in three quarters of an hour.[†] These, and numerous other cases, illustrate the intensely

---

[*] Wormley, Micro-chemistry of Poisons, 2nd ed., pp. 434, 435.

[†] Ibid, pp. 436, 437.

poisonous nature of tobacco. The evil effects of the repeated use of small amounts of tobacco, in smoking or chewing are also well understood.

It was in 1828, about five years before Joseph Smith's doctrine with respect to tobacco was given, **Joseph Smith probably did not know the poisonous nature of tobacco in 1833.** that nicotine was obtained in a pure state. Many years later the chemists and physiologists learned to understand the dangerous nature of the tobacco poison. It does not seem probable that Joseph Smith had heard of the discovery of nicotine in 1833; the discovery was announced in a German scientific journal, and in those days of few newspapers, scientific news, even of public interest, was not made generally known as quickly as is the case today. In fact, Hyrum Smith, the brother of the Prophet, on May 29, 1842, delivered a sermon upon the Word of Wisdom in which he says, "Tobacco is a nauseous, stinking, abominable thing;"* but nothing worse, thus basing his main objection to it on the revealed word of the Lord. Had Joseph and his associates been familiar with the isolation of nicotine and its properties, they would undoubtedly have mentioned it in sermons especially directed against the use of tobacco. In any case, at a time when it was but vaguely known that tobacco contained a poisonous principle, it would have been extremely hazardous for the reputation of an impostor to have claimed a revelation from God, stating distinctly the injurious effects of tobacco.

* The Contributor, vol. iv., p. 13;   Improvement Era, Vol. 4. pp. 943-9.

It should also be noted that Joseph Smith says that when tobacco is used for bruises and all sick cattle, it should be used with judgment and skill, thus impressing caution even in the external application of the herb. This is fully borne out by facts, for it has been found that "the external application of tobacco to abraded surfaces, and even to the healthy skin, has been attended with violent symptoms, and even death."*

In the matter of the chemistry and physiological action of tobacco, then, the Prophet, in 1833, was in full accord with the best knowledge of 1908. In the emphasis of his doctrine, he even anticipated the world of science.

"And again, hot drinks are not for the body or belly."†

When this statement was made, in 1833, the meaning of the expresson hot drinks was not clearly **The doctrine that** understood. Many believed that the **tea and coffee** only meaning of the above statement **are injurious** **to man is** was that drinks that are hot enough to **scientific.** burn the mouth should not be used. Others, however, claimed for the doctrine a deeper meaning. To settle the difficulty, appeal was made to Joseph Smith who explained that tea, coffee and similar drinks were meant by the expression hot drinks. From that time on, the Church has taught that tea and coffee should not be used by mankind.‡

---

* Wormley, Micro-chemistry of Poisons, p. 436.

† Doctrine and Covenants, 89: 9.

‡ See The Contributor, vol. iv. p. 13; Improvement Era, vol 4, pp. 943-9.

In the year 1821, several chemists isolated from coffee a bitter principle, of peculiar properties, which was named caffein. In 1827, the same substance was found to occur in tea. Numerous analysis show that there are between one and two per cent of caffein in coffee, and between three and six percent in tea. Later investigations have shown that caffein belongs to the vegetable poisons, and that its poisonous action is very strong.

Among the medical properties of caffein are the following, " in doses of three to five grains, it produces a peculiar wakefulness—after a dose of twelve grains, it produces intense physical restlessness and mental anxiety. Upon the muscles it acts as a powerful poison—it is used in medicines as a brain and heart stimulant."[*] Fatal cases of poisoning are also on record.

Caffein is not in any sense a food, but, as a stimulant, must be classed with tobacco, opium and other similar substances. Owing to its action on the heart and circulation, the body becomes heated, and in that sense a solution of caffein is a "hot drink." The use of tea and coffee in health is now generally condemned by the best informed persons in and out of the medical profession. Dr. W. Gilman Thompson says, "The continuance of the practice of drinking coffee to keep awake soon results in forming a coffee or tea habit, in which the individual becomes a slave to the beverage. * * * Muscular tremors are developed, with nervousness, anxiety, dread of impending evil, palpitation, heartburn, dyspepsia and insomnia. * * * It produces

---

[*] U. S. Dispensatory, 17th ed., pp. 278 and 279.

great irritability of the whole nervous system and one may even overexcite the mind."* While it is true that one cup of coffee or tea does not contain enough caffein to injure the system, yet the continual taking of these small doses results in a weakening of the whole system, that frequently leads to premature death.

The U. S. Consular and Trade Report for January, 1906,† warns against the use of coffee in the following words, "The important connection between consumption of coffee and epilepsy which deserves to be known everywhere, serves as a warning to be extremely careful with coffee made of beans containing caffein, and at any rate, children should be deprived of it entirely, otherwise their health will be exposed to great danger."

Besides caffein, both tea and coffee contain an astringent known as tannic acid. In coffee this substance is present only in small quantity, but in tea from four to twelve per cent occurs. Tannic acid is the substance found in oak bark, and has the property of making animal tissues hard—that is, makes leather of them. The habitual tea drinker subjects the delicate lining of the stomach and intestines to the action of this powerful drug.

Without going into further details, it is readily seen that the teachings of Joseph Smith, in 1833, in relation to the value of tea and coffee in human drinks, harmonizes with the knowledge of today. Moreover, he was in advance, in the certainty of his expressions, of the scientists of his day. It is true that caffein had been found in coffee and tea a few

---

* Practical Dietetics, p. 199.   † Page 249.

years before the revelation of 1833, but the physiological action of the drug was not known until many years afterwards. Besides, as in the case of tobacco, the Church leaders in speaking against the use of tea and coffee did not mention the poisonous principle that had recently been discovered in them; thus revealing their ignorance of the matter.

"And again, * * * all wholesome herbs God hath ordained for the constitution, nature, and use of man. Every herb in the season thereof, and every fruit in the season thereof; all these to be used with prudence and thanksgiving."*

The doctrines regarding the values of herbs and fruits harmonize with recent scientific truths.

This doctrine, which seems self-evident now, also evidences the divine inspiration of the Prophet Joseph. At the time this revelation was given, food chemistry was not understood; and, in fact, it was not until about 1860, that the basis upon which rests our knowledge of food chemistry, was firmly established. We now know that every plant contains four great classes of compounds: mineral substances, fats, sugars and starches, and protein, or the flesh-forming elements. We further know that no plant can live and grow without containing these groups of nutrients. It is also well understood that these substances are necessary for the food of the animal body, and that animal tissues are, themselves, composed of these groups, though in different proportions. In short, it has long been an established fact of science that any plant that does not contain a poisonous principle, may by proper cooking be used as a food for man.

---

* Doctrine and Covenants 89: 10, 11.

When Joseph Smith wrote, this was a daring suggestion to make, for there was absolutely no fact aside from popular experience, upon which to base the conclusion. The qualifying phrase, "all wholesome herbs," undoubtedly refers to the existence of classes of plants like coffee, tea, tobacco, etc., which contain some special principle injurious to the health.

"Yea, flesh also of beasts and of the fowls of the air, I, the Lord, have ordained for the use of man with thanksgiving; nevertheless they are to be used sparingly; and it is pleasing unto me that they should not be used only in times of winter, or of cold, or of famine."*

The doctrine concerning the use of meats is scientific.

The breadth of this doctrine lies in the fact that it is not absolutely forbidden to eat meat, as in all probability a fanatic, guided by his own wisdom, might have done; yet it must be observed, the implication is clear that it is possible for man to live without meat. Vegetarianism had been taught and practiced long before the days of Joseph Smith; but there had been no direct, positive proof that plants contain all the substances necessary for the sustenance of life. As stated above, it is now known that every class of nutritive substance found in meat is also found in plants. This is in full harmony with the implied meaning of Joseph Smith in the statement regarding the abstaining from meat.

"All grain is ordained for the use of man and of beasts, to be the staff of life. * * * All grain

---

* Doctrine and Covenants, 89: 12, 13.

The distinction between the values of grains is also scientific. is good for the food of man, as also the fruit of the vine, that which yieldeth fruit, whether in the ground or above the ground.   Nevertheless, wheat for man, and corn for the ox, and oats for the horse, and rye for the fowls and for swine, and for all beasts of the field, and barley for all useful animals, and for mild drinks, as also other grain."[*]

The first part of this teaching, that all grain can be used by man and beast, corresponds to the earlier statement that all wholesome plants may be used by man. The latter part respecting the best grain for certain classes of animals, is of a different nature and merits special consideration. As already mentioned, all plants and plant parts contain four great groups of nutritive substances. The relative proportions of these grains are different in different plants or plant parts. For instance, wheat contains about 71.9 per cent of starch and sugar; corn, 70.2 per cent; oats, 59.7 per cent; rye, 72.5 per cent; and barley, 69.8 per cent. Wheat contains about 11.9 per cent of protein or the flesh-forming elements; corn, 11.4 per cent; oats, 11.8 per cent; rye, 10.6 per cent; and barley 12.4 per cent.[†] It has further been demonstrated that a man or beast doing heavy work, requires a larger proportion of starch and sugar in his dietary than does one which has less work to do. Likewise, different classes of animals require different proportions of the various nutrients, not only through life but at the various periods of their lives. This principle has been recog-

---

[*] Doctrine and Covenants, 89: 14, 16 and 17.

[†] The Feeding of Animals, Jordan, p. 424.

nized so fully that during the last thirty-five or forty years the attention of experimenters has been directed toward the elucidation of laws which would make known the best combinations of foods for the various classes of farm animals, as well as for man. It must also be remarked that recent discoveries in science are showing more deep-seated differences in the composition of grains, than those here mentioned, as also corresponding differences in various classes of animals. Science will soon throw more light on this subject, and in all probability will confirm the views of Joseph Smith, with respect to the grain best adapted to certain animals.

A thoughtful reading of the above quotation clearly shows that Joseph Smith recognized the fundamental truth of food chemistry; namely, that while all plants contain the elements necessary for animal growth, yet the proportions of these elements are so different as to make some plants better adapted than others to a certain class of animals. That the ''Mormon'' prophet should have enunciated this principle from twenty to thirty years in advance of the scientific world, must excite wonder in the breast of any person, be he follower or opponent of Joseph Smith.

The discussion of the important statements made in section 89 of the book of *Doctrine and Covenants,* might be elaborated into a volume. The merest outline has been given here. The physiological teachings of the prophet concerning work, cleanliness and sleep, might also be considered with profit.

To summarize the contents of this chapter: Joseph Smith clearly recognized and taught the

Joseph Smith anticipated the world of science in the word of wisdom. physiological value of alcohol, tobacco, tea and coffee, at a time when scientific discoveries were just beginning to reveal the active principles of these commodities. The probability is that he knew nothing of what the world of science was doing in this direction, at the time the doctrine was taught. Joseph Smith clearly recognized and taught the fundamental truths of food chemistry, and the food relation of vegetable products to man, nearly a generation before scientists had arrived at the same doctrine. Whence came his knowledge?

Chapter XIV.

THE LAW OF EVOLUTION.

To every intelligence the question concerning the purpose of all things must at some time present itself. Every philosophical system has for its ultimate problem the origin and the destiny of the universe. Whence? Where?—the queries which arise before every human soul, and which have stimulated the truth-seekers of every age in their wearisome task of searching out nature's laws. Intelligent man cannot rest satisfied with the recognition of the forces at work in the universe, and the nature of their actions; he must know, also, the resultant of the interaction of the forces, or how the whole universe is affected by them; in short, man seeks the law of laws, by the operation of which, things have become what they are, and by which their destiny is controlled. This law when once discovered, is the foundation of religion as well as of science, and will explain all phenomena.

It was well toward the beginning of the last century before philosophical doctrines rose above mere speculation, and were based upon the actual observation of phenomena. As the scientific method of gathering facts and reasoning from them became established, it was observed that in all probability the great laws

Whence?
Where?

The only rational philosophy is based on science.

---

* Loc. cit., p. 550.   † Loc. cit., p. 564.

5

of nature were themselves controlled by some greater law. While many attempts have been made to formulate this law, yet it must be confessed, frankly, that only the faintest outline of it is possesesd by the world of science.

The sanest of modern philosophers, and the one who most completely attempted to follow the method of science in philosophical writings, was Herbert Spencer. Early in his life, he set himself the task of constructing a system of philosophy which should be built upon man's reliable knowledge of nature. A long life permitted him to realize this ambition. Though his works are filled with conclusions which cannot be accepted by most men, yet the facts used in his reasoning are authentic. By the world at large, the philosophy of Herbert Spencer is considered the only philosophy that harmonizes with the knowledge of today.

After having discussed, with considerable fullness, the elements of natural phenomena, such as **All things are** space, time, matter, motion and force, **continually chang-** Mr. Spencer concludes that all evidence **ing.—This is the** agrees in showing that "every object, **foundation of** **evolution.** no less than the aggregate of objects, undergoes from instant to instant some alteration of state."* That is to say that while the universe is one of system and order, no object remains exactly as it is, but changes every instant of time.

In two directions only can this ceaseless change affect an object; it either becomes more complex or more simple; it moves forward or backward; it grows or decays. In the words of Spencer, "All

---

* First Principles, p. 287.

things are growing or decaying, accumulating matter or wearing away, integrating or disintegrating.''* This, then, is the greatest known fundamental law of the universe, and of all things in it—that nothing stands still, but either progresses (evolution), or retrogrades (dissolution). Now, it has been found that under normal conditions all things undergo a process of evolution; that is, become more complex, or advance.† This, in its essence, is the law of evolution, about which so much has been said during the last fifty years. Undoubtedly, this law is correct, and in harmony with the known facts of the universe. It certainly throws a flood of light upon the phenomena of nature; though of itself, it tells little of the force behind it, in obedience to which it operates.

Spencer himself most clearly realized the insufficiency of the law of evolution alone, for he asks, ''May we seek for some all-pervading principle which underlies this all pervading process?''‡ and proceeds to search out this ''all-pervading principle'' which at last he determines to be the persistence of force—the operation of the universal, indestructible, incomprehensible force, which appears as gravitation, light, heat, electricity, magnetism, chemical affinity and in other forms.||

A natural question now is, Is there any limit to the changes undergone by matter, and which we designate as evolution? ''Will they go on forever? or will there be an end to them?''** As far as our

---

*Loc. cit., p. 292.   † Loc. cit., p. 337.

‡ First Principles, p. 408. || Loc. cit., p. 494

** Loc. cit., p. 496.

knowledge goes, there is an end to all things, a death which is the greatest known change, and as far as human experience goes, all things tend toward a death-like state of rest. That this rest is permanent is not possible under the law of evolution; for it teaches that an ulterior process initiates a new life; that there are alternate eras of evolution and dissolution. "And thus there is suggested the conception of a past during which there have been successive evolutions analogous to that which is now going on; and a future during which successive other such evolutions may go on ever the same in principle but never the same in concrete result."* This is practically the same as admitting eternal growth.

Evolution does not admit a final death.

The final conclusion is that "we can no longer contemplate the visible creation as having a definite beginning or end, or as being isolated. It becomes unified with all existence before and after; and the force which the universe presents falls into the same category with space and time, as admitting of no limitation in thought."†

It is interesting to note the conclusion concerning spirit and matter, to which Mr. Spencer is led by the law of evolution. "The materialist and spiritualist controversy is a mere war of words, in which the disputants are equally absurd—each thinking that he understands that which it is impossible for any man to understand. Though the relation of subject and object renders necessary to us these antithetical conceptions of spirit and matter; the one is no less than

Spirit and matter are alike.

the other to be regarded as but a sign of the Unknown Reality which underlies both."[*]

While the law of evolution, as formulated by Spencer and accepted by the majority of modern thinkers, is the nearest approach to the truth possessed by the world of science, yet there is no disposition on the part of the writer to defend the numerous absurdities into which Spencer and his followers have fallen when reasoning upon special cases.

Many years before Mr. Spencer's day, it had been suggested, vaguely, that advancement seemed to be the great law of nature. Students of botany and zoology were especially struck by this fact, for they observed how animals and plants could be made to change and improve under favorable conditions, by the intervention of man's protection. In 1859, Mr. Charles Darwin published a theory to account for such variation, in which he assumed that there is a tendency on the part of all organisms to adapt themselves to their surroundings, and to change their characteristics, if necessary, in this attempt. He further showed that in the struggle for existence among animals and plants, the individual best fitted for its environment usually survives. These facts, Mr. Darwin thought, led to a process of natural selection, by which, through long ages, deep changes were caused in the structure of animals. In fact, Darwin held that the present-day plants and animals have descended from extinct and very different

Evolution and natural selection do not necessarily go together.

---

*First Principles, pp. 570 and 572.

ancestors.* The experiences of daily life bear out the assertion that organic forms may be changed great-ly—witness the breeding of stock and crops, prac-ticed by all intelligent farmers—and all in all the theory seemed so simple that numerous biologists im-mediately adopted it, and began to generalize upon it. Having once accepted the principle that the present-day species have descended from very unlike an-cestors, it was easy to asume that all organic nature had descended from one common stock.   It was claimed that man, in a distant past, was a monkey; still earlier, perhaps, a reptile; still earlier a fish, and so on.   From that earliest form, man had be-come what he is by a system of natural selection.   In spite of the absence of proofs, such ideas became cur-rent among the scientists of the day.   In this view was included, of course, the law of evolution or growth, and thus, too, the law became associated with the notion that man has descended from the lower animals.   In fact, however, the law of evolu-tion is just as true, whether or not Darwin's theory of natural selection be adopted.

In justice to Darwin, it should be said that he in nowise claimed that natural selection was alone sufficient to cause the numerous changes in organic form and life; but, on the contrary, held that it is only one means of modification.†

Professor Huxley, who, from early manhood, was an eminent and ardent supporter of the Darwin-ian hypothesis frankly says, "I adopt Mr. Darwin's

---

* Origin of Species, p. 6.

† Origin of Species, p. 6; also Darwin and After Dar-win Romanes, Vol. II. pp. 2-6.

hypothesis, therefore, subject to the production of proof that physiological species may be produced by selective breeding; and for the reason that it is the only means at present within reach of reducing the chaos of observed facts to order.''* After writing a book to establish the descent of man from apes, Professor Huxley is obliged to confess that ''the fossil remains of man hitherto discovered do not seem to take us appreciably nearer to that lower pithecoid form, by the modification of which he has, probably, become what he is.''†

This is not the place to enter into this famous controversy. The relation of the theory of natural selection to the law of evolution is not established; that man and the great classes of animals and plants have sprung from one source is far from having been proved; that the first life came upon this earth by chance is as unthinkable as ever. Even at the present writing, recent discoveries have been reported which throw serious doubt upon natural selection as an all-sufficient explanation of the wonderful variety of nature. The true scientific position of the Darwinian hypothesis is yet to be determined.

The moderate law of evolution which claims that all normal beings are advancing, without asserting that one form of life can pass into another, is, however, being more and more generally accepted, for it represents an eternal truth, of which every new discovery bears evidence.

Were it not that the law of evolution is of such fundamental value in the understanding of natural

---

* Man's Place in Nature, p. 128.   † Loc. cit., p. 183.

phenomena, it would hardly be expected that the calling of Joseph Smith would necessitate any reference to it. Besides, upwards of fifteen years elapsed after the martyrdom of Joseph and Hyrum Smith before the world of science conceived the hypothesis. **Joseph Smith taught the law of eternal growth—evolution.** One of the leading doctrines of the Church resembles the spirit of the law of universal growth so nearly that one is forced to believe that the great truth embodied by this doctrine is the truth shadowed forth by the law of evolution.

The doctrine of God, as taught by Joseph Smith, is the noblest of which the human mind can conceive. No religion ascribes to God more perfect attributes than does that of the Latter-day Saints. Yet the Church, asserts that God was not always what he is today. Through countless ages he has grown towards greater perfection, and at the present, though in comparison with humankind, he is omniscient and omnipotent, he is still progressing. Of the beginning of God, we have no record, save that he told his servant Abraham, "I came down in the beginning in the midst of all the intelligences thou hast seen."[*]

As told by Joseph Smith, in May, 1833, John the Apostle said of God, Jesus Christ, "And I, John, saw that he received not of the fulness at first, but continued from grace to grace, until he received a fulness; and thus he was called the Son of God, because he received not of the fulness at first."[†]

Man, likewise, is to develop until, in comparison with his present condition, he becomes a God. For

---

[*] Book of Abraham, 3: 21.

[†] Doctrine and Covenants, 93: 12-14.

instance, in speaking of the salvation to which all men who live correct lives shall attain, the Prophet says, "For salvation consists in the glory, authority, majesty, power and dominion which Jehovah pos-

Man will develop until he becomes like God.

sesses;"[*] and in another place, "Then shall they be Gods, because they have no end; therefore shall they be from everlasting to everlasting, because they continue; then shall they be above all, because all things are subject unto them. Then shall they be Gods, because they have all power."[†]

That this is not a sudden elevation, but a gradual growth, is evident from many of the writings of Joseph Smith, of which the following are illustrations. "He that receiveth light and continueth in God, receiveth more light, and that light groweth brighter and brighter until the perfect day."[‡] "For if you keep my commandments you shall receive of his fulness, and be glorified in me as I am in the Father; therefore, I say unto you, you shall receive grace for grace."[§]

In various sermons Joseph Smith enlarged upon the universal principle of advancement, but few of them have been preserved for us. In a sermon delivered in April, 1844, the following sentences occur, "God himself was once as we are now, and is an exalted Man, and sits enthroned in yonder heavens. You have got to learn how to be Gods yourselves, and to be kings and priests to God, the same as all Gods have done before you; namely, by going from

---

[*] Doctrine and Covenants, Lectures on Faith, 7: 8.

[†] Doctrine and Covenants, 132: 20.

[‡] Ibid., 50: 24.   [§] Ibid., 93: 20.

one small degree to another, and from a small capacity to a great one; from grace to grace, from exaltation to exaltation.''*

The preceding quotations suffice to show that with regard to man, Joseph Smith taught a doctrine

Joseph Smith anticipated science in the statement of the law of evolution.
of evolution which in grandeur and extent surpasses the wildest speculations of the scientific evolutionist. Yet Joseph Smith taught this doctrine as one of eternal truth, taught him by God. There can be no doubt that the truth behind Spencer's law of evolution, and the doctrine taught by the ''Mormon'' prophet, are the same. The great marvel is that Joseph Smith, who knew not the philosophies of men, should have anticipated by thirty years or more the world of science in the enunciation of the most fundamental law of the universe of living things.

Now, it is true that Joseph Smith did not extend this law to the lower animals; but it must be

Animals are subject to evolution.
remembered that his mission on earth was to teach a system of redemption for men. Yet, it is an interesting observation that he taught that men and animals had a spiritual existence, before they were placed on earth. ''For I, the Lord God, created all things of which I have spoken, spiritually, before they were naturally upon the face of the earth. And out of the ground made I, the Lord God, to grow every tree, naturally, that is pleasant to the sight of man; and man could behold it. And it became also a living soul. For it was spiritual in the day that I created it; for it re-

---

* Contributor, vol. 4, pp. 254 and 255.

maineth in the sphere in which I, God, created it.''*

If, in common with men, animals and plants were created spiritually, it may not be an idle speculation that the lower forms of life will advance, in their respective fields, as man advances in his. However, a statement in the above quotation must not be overlooked, "It remaineth in the sphere in which I, God, created it." This would preclude any notion that by endless development a plant may become an animal, or that one of the lower classes of animals become a high animal, or a man. Is not this the place where, perhaps, the evolution of science has failed? All things advance, but each order of creation within its own sphere. There is no jumping from order to order. The limits of these orders are yet to be found.

Spencer's belief that one period of evolution follows another† is brought strongly to mind in contemplating the doctrine of Joseph Smith that man, and other things, had first a spiritual existence, now an earthly life, then a higher existence after death. Is not the parallelism strong—and may it not be that here, also, the "Mormon" prophet could have shown the learned philosopher the correct way?

Finally, one other suggestion must be made. Spencer, after a long and involved argument, con-

God is the compelling power of evolution. cludes (or proves as he believes) that the great law of evolution is a necessity that follows from the law of the persistence of force. In chapter two of this series, the

---

* Book of Moses, 3: 5 and 9.   See also Doctrine and Covenants, 29: 31, 32.

† First Principles, p. 550.

scientific conception of the persistence of force was identified with the operations of the Holy Spirit, as taught by Joseph Smith. This Spirit is behind all phenomena; by it as a medium, God works his will with the things of the universe, and enables man to move on to eternal salvation, to advance, and become a God; every law is of necessity a result of the operation of this Spirit. Here, again, the "Mormon" prophet anticipated the world of science; and his conceptions are simpler and more direct than those invented by the truth-seekers, who depended upon themselves and their own powers.

Marvelous is this view of the founder of "Mormonism." Where did he learn in his short life, amidst sufferings and persecution such as few men have known, the greatest mysteries of the universe!

Chapter XV.

THE PLAN OF SALVATION.

In the preceding chapter the law of evolution was shown to be the cementing law of nature, which **Why am I on earth?** explains the destiny of man. To live is to change, and (if the change is right) to grow. Through all the ages to come righteous man will increase in complexity and will grow towards a condition of greater knowledge, greater power and greater opportunity.

While the great law of evolution may be quite sufficient for the general survey, it does not explain the special conditions amidst which organized intelligences find themselves. Man asks, Why am I on earth? Science is silent. Up to the present time, many scientific men have not found it necessary to postulate an intelligent force behind the phenomena of nature, which would explain our earthly existence.

The Mormon answer to this question lies in the Mormon doctrine of the plan of salvation. There can be no attempt to harmonize the Mormon plan with that of science, for science has none; but, that the Mormon plan of salvation is strictly scientific, and rests upon the irrevocable laws of the universe can certainly be demonstrated.

Fundamental, in the doctrines of Joseph, is the statement that all intelligence is eternal; and that God at the best is the organizer of the spirits of men. The ether of science has been compared with the Holy Spirit of Mormonism. The spirit body may be likened to an ether body of man, and is the condition of his original existence. From the original condition, at man's spiritual birth, under the law of evolution he has steadily grown in complexity, which means in power.

Perfection comes only when matter, spirit and intelligence are associated.

In the universe are recognized ether or spirit, force or intelligence, and matter. Matter may act upon the ether and the ether upon matter; but ether acts most effectively upon ether, and matter upon matter. The original man, in whom intelligence and other forces acted through a purely spiritual or ether body, could impress matter and be impressed by it only in part. The man was imperfect because he did not touch directly the world of matter, and could know only in part the phenomena of the material world, which forms an integral part of the universe. In the words of Joseph Smith, ''Spirit and element inseparably connected, receiveth a fullness of joy, and when separated, man can not receive a fullness of joy.''*

For man's perfection, it then became necessary that his spiritual body should be clothed with a material one, and that he should become as familiar with the world of matter, as he had become with the world of spirit. God, as the supreme intelligence, who desired all other spirits to know and become mighty, led in the formulation of the plan, whereby they should obtain knowledge of all the contents of the universe.

---

* Doctrine and Covenants, 93: 33, 34.

For the purpose of perfecting the plan, a council of the Gods, or perfected intelligences was called. **The fall of Adam necessary to perfect intelligence.** It was decided to organize an earth from available materials, and place the spirits on it, clothed with bodies of the grosser elements. An esesntial function of intelligence is free agency; and that the spirits might have the fullest opportunity to exercise this agency in their earthly career, they were made to forget the events of their spiritual existence. To learn directly the nature of grossest matter, the earth bodies of necessity were made subject to the process of the disintegration called death.

To make possible the subjection of eternal, spiritual organized intelligences to perishable, material structures, certain natural laws would naturally be brought into operation. From the point of view of the eternal spirit, it might mean the breaking of a law directed towards eternal life; yet to secure the desired contact with matter, the spirit was compelled to violate the law. Thus, in this earth life, a man who desires to acquire a first hand acquaintance with magnetism and electricity, may subject himself to all kinds of electric shocks, that, perhaps, will affect his body injuriously; yet, for the sake of securing the experience, he may be willing to do it. Adam, the first man, so used natural laws that his eternal, spiritual body became clothed upon with an earthly body, subject to death. Then in begetting children, he was able to produce earthly bodies for the waiting spirits.

According to this doctrine, the socalled Fall of

Adam was indispensable to the evolving of organized intelligences that should have a complete acquaintance with all nature, and a full control over their free agencies. If laws were broken, it was done because of the heroism of the first parents, and not because of their sinfulness.

Mormon theology does not pretend to say in what precise manner Adam was able to secure his corruptible body; neither is science able to answer all the "whys' suggested by recorded experiences. The doctrines of Joseph Smith maintain, however, that the events connected with the introduction of organized intelligences on this earth, were in full accord with the simple laws governing the universe. That the Mormon view of this matter, so fundamental in every system of theology, is rational, can not be denied.

However, the bodies given to the spirits continued for only a few years; then they were dis-

The atonement was in harmony with natural law. organized in death. Adam's work had been done well. After the death of the mortal body, the spirit was still without a permanent body of matter, that would complete his contact with the elements of the universe. Therefore, it was necessary to bring other laws into operation, that would reorganize these dead material bodies in such a way that they would no longer be subject to the forces of disorganization, death and decay. The eternal spiritual body, united with this eternal material body, then constituted a suitable home for eternal intelligence, whereby it might be able, under the law of evolution to attain the greatest conceivable knowledge and power.

The personage who directed the laws that cancelled the necessary work of Adam, and made the corruptible body incorruptible was the Savior, Jesus Christ. As Adam, by his personal work, made the earth career possible for all who succeeded him; so Jesus, by His personal work, made it possible for the spirits to possess immortal material bodies.

Conditions that may be likened to the atonement are found in science. Suppose an electrical current, supplying a whole city with power and light, is passing through a wire. If for any reason the wire is cut the city becomes dark and all machines driven by the current cease their motion. To restore the current, the ends of the broken wire must be reunited. If a person, in his anxiety to restore the city to its normal conditions, seizes the ends of the wire with his bare hands, and unites them, he probably will receive the full charge of the current in his body. Yet, as a result, the light and power will return to the city; and one man by his action, has succeeded in doing the work for many.

The actual method by which Jesus was enabled to make mortal bodies immortal, is not known to us. Neither can we understand just why the shedding of the Savior's blood was necessary for the accomplishment of this purpose. Like the work of Adam, the exact nature of the atonement is unknown. Still, throughout this plan of Salvation, every incident and accomplished fact are strictly rational. There is no talk of a God, who because of his own will, and in opposition to natural laws, placed man on earth.

The presence of organized intelligences in earth

is simply a link in the evolution of man. The plan of salvation is the method whereby the evolution of man is furthered. The intelligence

Earth life is a link in man's evolution.

who conforms to the Plan, at last attains salvation, which means eternal life and endless development, directed by the free agency of an organized intelligence clothed with an incorruptible body of spirit and matter.

Can any other system of theology produce an explanation of the presence of man on earth, which connects earthly life with the time before and the time after, on the basis of the accepted laws of the universe?

Flawless seems the structure reared by the Mormon Prophet. Had he been an imposter, human imperfection would have revealed itself somewhere.*

---

* It must not be assumed that in this chapter has been given a full account of the Mormon doctrine of the Atonement. These essays are not in any sense a full exposition of Mormon theology.

Chapter XVI.

THE SIXTH SENSE.

The five senses are the great gateways through which all the knowledge in man's possession has been obtained. Examine the matter as we may, the truth of this statement persists. By seeing, hearing, smelling, tasting and feeling, only, is man brought into contact with external nature and himself, and is furnished material upon which the intellect can act. True it is, that the sense of feeling may be divided into a number of poorly known sub-senses, of which that of touch is the best known, but, probably, these are very nearly related, and we may still maintain the existence of the *five* senses of man.

The six senses, need help to reorganize many phenomena of nature.

Wonderful as these senses are, yet, in the presence of many natural phenomena, they are very weak, and require help, in order that the operations of nature may be recognized. Take, as an illustration, the refined sense of sight. Light, coming from a distant star, is readily recognized; the same quantity of light coming from a house, half a mile distant, is even more distinctly sensed by the eye. In both these cases, though the light is recognized, the sensation is not so sharply defined as to produce a distinct image of the star or of the house. To make the images of distant objects distinct, the telescope has been invented; and this instrument is a most important aid to the sense of sight. The microscope is a similar aid to the eye, by which the light-rays coming from minute objects are so bent and arranged that the object appears magnified, and may be sensed in its details by the eye. The ear-trumpet is a similar device for collecting, concentrating and defining sound waves that ordinarily would be, to the ear, a confusion of sounds. The ear-trumpet is a mighty help to the sense of hearing.

The light which passes through the lenses of the telescope and microscope, is the light which is ordinarily recognized by the eye. The instruments effect no change in the light; they merely arrange the waves so as to produce a clear and distinct outline of the objects from which the light comes. Likewise, the sound waves entering the ear-trumpet are in nowise changed in their essential nature, but are simply rearranged or concentrated to produce a more definite impression on the ear. Instruments similar to those here mentioned are the simplest aids to man's senses.

With respect to many forces of nature, the unaided senses of man are helpless. The subtle force of magnetism, for instance, appears incapable of affecting directly any of the senses. A person may hold a powerful lodestone in his hand and feel no influence different from that coming from a piece of sandstone. A person may work near a wire carrying a current of electricity, and, though it is well known that peculiar conditions exist in the universal ether around such a wire, yet, through his five senses, he may never become aware of the existence of this current. A piece of uranium ore, as has been found in recent years, emits various kinds of rays related to the now famous X- or Roentgen rays, yet no indication comes directly through any of the five senses that such is the case. In fact, men of science worked with the ores of uranium for many years before discovering the emission of ether waves. In the light which comes from the sun are numerous forms of energy that do not directly affect the senses, and therefore remained unknown for many centuries. Numerous other illustrations might be quoted to show the existence of natural forces that are beyond the direct recognition of man. In the great ocean of the unknown, lie, undoubtedly, countless forces that shall never be known by a direct action upon the senses of man.*

As is well understood, however, even these apparently unknowable manifestations of nature may be known, if proper aids be secured. In every case the problem is this: To obtain some medium, be it natural or manufactured, which transforms the unknown force into a known force, that is capable of affecting the senses of man. The search for such media is one of the most important labors of science.

---

* The writer is aware of the beliefs held by many students regarding the so-called touch sense, heat sense, magnetic sense, electrical sense, spiritual sense, etc. So little is known of these subdivisions of the sense of feeling, that they are not considered in this popular writing. There is, moreover, no evidence that the magnetic sense, as an example, if it exists, is a direct effect of magnetic forces; it is as easily believed that the body somehow converts magnetic forces, under certain circumstances, into other forces that may be sensed by man.

For instance, sunlight has been known from the beginning of the human race, and its nature has been studied by almost every genera- tion of thinkers. To the time of New- ton, it was only white light—or little more. Newton discovered that if a ray of white light be allowed to fall upon a triangular prism of glass, it is dispersed or broken into a number of colored rays known as the spectrum. All sunlight, passed through a glass prism, produces this colored spectrum; and the colors are arranged invariably in the same order; namely from violet through the intermediate colors to red. By passing this spec- trum through another prism, white light is pro- duced. Sunlight was thus proved to consist of a number of kinds of colored light. The eye alone is incapable of resolving white light into its elements: the glass prism thus becomes an aid to the sense of sight, by which a new domain of science is laid open to view.

The advance of knowledge requires instru- ments that con- vert natural phenomena into intelligible forms. Thus the un- known is re- vealed.

Above the red end of the spectrum, obtained from white light, nothing is visible, yet if a delicate thermometer be placed there, the increase in tem- perature shows the presence of certain invisible heat rays, and by moving the thermometer, it may be shown that the invisible heat spectrum is longer than the light spectrum itself. This, again, makes known to man a world that the five senses can recognize only with difficulty; and in this case, the thermometer is the necessary aid.

Even more interesting is the violet end of the spectrum. Like the red end, it is invisible. In fact, for centuries it was believed that the light spectrum represented the whole spectrum. During the last century it was found that if a photographic plate be placed below the violet end of the spectrum, it is affected by invisible light rays, which are popularly denominated chemical rays. By placing the photographic plate in various positions, it has been discovered that the chemical spectrum is as long as the visible part. Since the days of Newton, therefore, the known part of the spectrum of sunlight has been trebled in length, and there is no certainty that all is now known concerning the matter. In this particular, the photographic plate has become a means of revealing an unknown world to the senses.

If a low tension current of electricity passes through a wire, it cannot be sensed directly by man; but if a delicately adjusted magnetic needle be placed above and parallel to such wire, the current will turn the needle to one side and keep it there. The magnetic needle then makes known the presence of a current of electricity which has no appreciable effect upon any of man's five senses. Similarly, the magnetic currents passing over the earth are not felt by man in such a way as to be recognized, but a magnetic needle, properly adjusted, will immediately assume an approximately north and south direction. in obedience to the pull of the magnetic currents.. In this manner the magnetic needle, again, reveals to man the existence and presence of forces that he cannot sense directly.

A piece of glass into which has been incorporated a small amout of the element uranium, is an instrument which reveals many wonders of the unsensed world.   If the uranium glass be brought near the violet end of the spectrum of sunlight, it immediately glows, because it has the power of changing the invisible chemical rays into ordinary, white light rays.   With such an instrument, darkness can be literally changed into light.   Similarly, many of the class of rays to which belong the X-rays, and which are dark to the eye, and do not directly affect any of the other senses, are converted by uranium glass into visible rays.   This glass, then, becomes another means whereby the world which does not directly affect our senses, may be made known.

The X- or Roentgen rays have been mentioned several times.   It is generally known that they have the power of passing through the body and various other opaque bodies.   The rays themselves are invisible, both before entering and after leaving the body; moreover, they do not affect any of the other senses of man.   Were it not that the power is possessed of changing these rays to light rays, man could know nothing of the Roentgen rays.   In fact, a screen, covered with powdered crystals of a chemical compound known as barium platinocyanide, is held behind the object through which the rays are passing, and the moment they touch this substance they are changed to light rays, and the screen glows. Or, instead, a photographic plate may be used, for the Roentgen rays affect the materials from which these plates are made.   The screen of barium platinocyanide is, therefore, another means for revealing the unknown world.

Such illustrations might be multiplied, but would add no strength to the discussion.   There is, however, another class of instruments which enable the senses to recognize natural forces that do not act

"Tuning" to establish sympathetic vibrations is a form of the aids for explaining the unknown.

directly upon the consciousness of man. If a musical note is produced on a violin, near a piano, the piano string which is stretched or tuned right, will give out the same note. The sound waves from the violin penetrate the piano, and the string which is tuned to give out the same note takes up the energy of the sound waves, and is set in vibration, with the result that the same note is given out by the piano. This is known as sympathetic vibrations. It is possible, therefore, to make a piano give out any note within its range, without any solid object touching the instrument. In the universal ether, which surrounds and penetrates all things, are numberless waves of all kinds, and of all vibrations. If the proper instrument be used, and tuned aright, it is possible to separate from this tumult of waves any desired kind or degree of wave motion, and to convert it into some known form of energy, say electricity.

This principle is used in modern wireless telegraphy. Electric waves are sent out by the operator with a certain rapidity. These waves radiate into space, in all directions, and are lost, apparently, in the confusion of myriads of other waves. Nevertheless, if the waves are not by some chance totally destroyed, it is possible to obtain them again, by the use of a receiving instrument which is tuned exactly the same as that used by the operator, at the station where the waves are sent out. A message sent from London may be received anywhere on earth where the receiving instruments are tuned aright; at the same time, if the peculiar note or vibration of the message is not known, so that the receivers can not be tuned properly, the message, though it be all about it, can never be received.

Such aids to our senses do not depend so much upon the nature of the material, as upon the degree to which it is brought into sympathy with the force to be recognized.

Now, though our senses are imperfect, and recognize only a small part of the phenomena of nature, yet it is very probable that, with such helps as have been described, nothing in nature need remain forever unknown. The means by which the forces of nature, that cannot be sensed directly, are brought to man's recognition may well be named, collectively, man's sixth sense.

With proper aids man's senses may discover the whole of nature.

The progress of science depends upon the discovery of aids to man's senses; a new and vast field is invariably opened whenever a new aid is discovered.

In the works of Joseph Smith, which teach that there is no real line of demarkation between the natural and spiritual worlds, it would be not surprising to find recognized the scientific principle, above discussed, that by the use of proper instruments, the world outside of the five senses, may be brought within man's consciousness.

Joseph Smith recognized the existence of media which render the unknown, known.

According to the story of Joseph Smith, he was first visited by an angel, September 21, 1823, when the Prophet was less than eighteen years of age.

Among other things, the angel told the boy that "there was a book deposited, written on gold plates," giving an account of the former inhabitants of the American continent; "also, that there were two stones in silver bows—and these stones, fastened to a breastplate, constituted what is called the Urim and Thummim—deposited with the plates; and the possession and use of these stones were what constituted 'Seers' in ancient or former times; and that God had prepared them for the purpose of translating the book."* This reference to the Urim and Thummim, and their purpose, makes it clear that the Prophet, at the beginning of his career, recognized (whether consciously or unconsciously we know not), the existence of means or media by which things unknown, such as a strange language, may be converted into forms that can reach the understanding.

When the actual work of translation began, the Urim and Thummim were found indispensable, and in various places the statement is made that the translation was made, "by means of the Urim and Thummim."† On one occasion, when the Prophet, through the defection of Martin Harris, lost a portion of the manuscript translation the Urim and Thummim were taken from him, and the power of translation ceased. Upon the return of the instruments the work was resumed.‡ While it is very probable that the Prophet was required to place

The Book of Mormon was translated by such aids—the Urim and Thummim.

---

* History of the Church, vol. 1, p. 12.

† Doctrine and Covenants, 10: 1.

‡ History of the Church, vol. 1, p. 23.

himself in the proper spiritual and mental attitude, before he could use the Urim and Thummim successfully, yet it must also be true that the stones were essential to the work of translation.

The Urim and Thummim were not used alone for translation, but most of the early revelations **Revelations** were obtained by their means. Speak-**were received** ing of those days, the Prophet usually **by such aids.** says: " I enquired of the Lord through the Urim and Thummim, and obtained the following."* The "stones in silver bows" seemed, therefore, to have possessed the general power of converting manifestations of the spiritual world into terms suitable to the understanding of Joseph Smith.

The doctrine of the use of the Urim and Thummim is in perfect harmony with the established law of modern science, that special media are necessary to bring the unknown world within the range of man's senses. To believers in the Bible, the use of the Urim and Thummim can offer no obstacles, and to those who possess a rational conception of God—that he is the Master of the universe, who works his will by natural means—it cannot be more difficult to believe that God's will may appear through the agency of special "stones in silver bows," than to concede that invisible ether waves, become luminous when they fall upon a piece of uranium glass. The virtue possessed by the latter glass is no more evident than is the virtue claimed by Joseph Smith to be possessed by the Urim and Thummim.

It is a noteworthy fact that the Prophet does not

---

* History of the Church, vol. 1, pp. 33, 36, 45, 49 and 53.

enter into an argument to prove the necessity of the use of the Urim and Thummim. Only in an incidental way, as he tells the straightforward story of his life, does he mention them; and with a simplicity that argues strongly for his veracity, does he assume that, of course, they were necessary and were used as he recounts. A shrewd imposter, building a great theological structure as is the Church founded by Joseph Smith, would have appreciated that difficult questions would be asked concerning the seer stones, and would have attempted to surround them with some explanation. Joseph Smith offers no defense for the use of these instruments; neither does the scientist excuse himself for using uranium glass, in the study of certain radiations.

The Prophet did not always receive his revelations by the assistance of the Urim and Thummim. As the Prophet placed himself in tune with the unknown, he became less dependent on external aids. As he grew in experience and understanding, he learned to bring his spirit into such an attitude that it became a Urim and Thummim to him, and God's will was revealed without the intervention of external means. This method is clearly, though briefly, expressed in one of the early revelations:

Behold, you have not understood; you have supposed that I would give it unto you, when you took no thought, save it was to ask me; but, behold, I say unto you, that you must study it out in your mind; then you must ask me if it be right, and if it is right, I will cause that your bosom shall burn within you; therefore, you shall feel that it is right; but if it be not right, you shall have no such feelings, but you shall have a stupor of thought, that cause you to forget the thing which is wrong.*

The essence of this statement is that if a person will concentrate his powers so as to come into harmony with God, truth will be revealed to him; and is not that like the tuning of a coil of wire so that it can take up the waves of certain lengths, that may be passing through the ether? If an inert mass of iron can be so tuned, can anyone refuse to believe that man, highly organized as he is, can "tune" himself to be in harmony with the forces of the universe? The universal ether of science is like the Holy Spirit, and the waves or energy of the ether is like the intelligent action of that Spirit controlled by God. Heat, light, magnetism, electricity, and the other forces, become, then, simply various forms of God's speech, any of which may be understood, if the proper means of interpretation is at hand.

The "testimony of the spirit" is scientific.

In the Book of Mormon, the Prophet states that "When ye shall receive these things, I would exhort you that ye would ask God, the Eternal Father, in the name of Christ, if these things are not true; and if ye shall ask with a sincere heart, with real intent, having faith in Chirst, he will manifest the truth of it unto you, by the power of the Holy Ghost; and by the power of the Holy Ghost ye may know the truth of all things."†

This involves the principle discussed above. By placing oneself in harmony with the requirements of the subject in hand, the truth must become known,

---

* Doctrine and Covenants, 9: 7-9.

† Moroni 10: 4, 5.

even as an instrument properly tuned must feel the influence of the ether waves with which it is in harmony.

Again, then, the conceptions of the Mormon Prophet rise to equal heights with the best theories of the scientists. In simple phrases, apparently unconscious of the philosophical meaning of the doctrines, Joseph Smith recognized the various means whereby man's senses may be enabled to seize upon and comprehend the natural forces which to man's unaided senses must remain unknown forever.

It cannot be justly claimed that the Prophet anticipated the world of science in the recognition of this principle, but reading his works in the light of modern progress, it cannot be denied that he placed a greater value upon the aids to man's senses, with respect to the subtle forces of the universe, than did any of his contemporaries. That acknowledgment is a wonderful tribute to the powers of an unlearned boy.

Evidence crowds upon evidence, and testimony upon testimony, until the opposition of logic falls away; and Joseph Smith rises above the fog of prejudice, a mighty prophet of our God.

Chapter XVII.

THE NATURE OF GOD.

In every philosophy of the universe, the question concerning the primary cause of the phenomena **Nearly all** of nature always arises. Ancient and **thinkers believe** modern philosophers, alike, have dis-**in God or an** cussed the probability of the existence **equivalent.** of this primary cause and its properties. Plato, putting the words into the mouth of Socrates, declares, "I do believe in the Gods."* Aristotle, the greatest of early thinkers, assumed that a God exists, from whom all other forces are derived. For example, "From a first principle, then, of this kind—I mean, one that is involved in the assumption of a First Mover—hath depended the Heaven and Nature."† Spencer, speaking in these latter days, likewise implies the existence of the equivalent of the God of men, thus, "If religion and science are to be reconciled, the basis of reconciliation must be this deepest, widest and most certain of all facts—that the Power which the universe manifests to us is utterly inscrutable."‡

To the great majority of men, in all ages, the idea of a God or Power, has appeared to be a necessity. Naturally, there has been a great variety of

---

* Plato, The Apology, chap. XXIV.

† Aristotle,, Metaphysics, chap. VII, sec. 4.

‡ First Principles, p. 48.

opinions concerning the nature of God, or the great Power behind things. Some, including the early Greek thinkers, looked upon God as a personal being of transcendental attributes; others gave Him a more shadowy form, and made of Him nothing more than an all pervading spiritual essence. Still others, considering the relations of all natural operations to the infinite power of God, identified Him with Nature, and then, with astonishing shortsight denied His personal existence. Thus, by degrees, arose the various theists, who accepted a personal God with varying attributes; the pantheists, who identified God with nature, and the atheists, who denied absolutely God, or any equivalent. Among those who have adopted the idea of God, the chief dispute has been largely as to His personality; to the atheists the essential consideration has been that the laws of nature are self-operative and need no directing force such as is implied in the conception of a God.

As modern science arose, certain conceptions became established which were directly related to the **Science points to a force of forces** idea of God. In obedience to the modern tendency towards simplification, the great variety in the material world has been referred to a few elements (nearly 80); and all the forces of nature are now held to be modes of motion of matter or of the one all pervading substance, the ether. The complexity of nature is produced by new combinations of matter, ether and motion. According to this doctrine, all the phenomena in the universe may be explained by referring them to the action of forces upon matter and ether. There is a limited number of elements, which, at the present, can not be converted into each other. There is only one ether, which can probably exist in various degrees of density. There are numerous forces, which may be converted into each other. Thus light may be changed into heat; heat into electricity and electricity into light again.

Scientists have long asked if there is one great universal force, of which all other forces are merely variations. Usually, the thinkers have agreed that the indications point to such a central force, which by many has been identified with gravitation. Newton and many of the men who followed him in the development of the theory of gravitation, agreed that probably the force of gravitation is the source of all other natural forces. Thus the doctrines of modern science point to *one* force from which all other forces are derived; and thus, the complexity of nature has been simplified, by explaining it on the assumption of this one force. Those who believe in God have claimed that this points to one great Being as the mover behind all things; the atheists have declared, that these scientific conceptions indicate that there is no real necessity for a God; and many honest searchers who have reached this closed door, have declared, "I do not know. It may be God; it may be force. It cannot be known."

"Mormonism" has harmonized science and theology in its conception of God. As has been shown earlier in this volume, Joseph Smith taught that the central force of the universe is intelligence.

"Mormonism" teaches that intelligence is the force of forces.

Gravitation, heat, light, magnetism, electricity, chemical attraction, are all various manifestations of the all-pervading force of intelligence. This, it may be seen, is the simple theory advanced by scientists, with the definition of the first force added.

The "Mormon" Prophet taught, further, that the individual is organized intelligence; that the organization is the instrument whereby intelligence may be concentrated, focussed and directed. Man is superior to beasts because his organization permits a greater use of the universal force of intelligence. Under the law of evolution, man's organization will become more and more complex. That is, he will increase in his power of using intelligence until in time, he will develop so far that, in comparison with his present state, he will be a God. Conversely, God, who is a superior organization, using and directing the force of intelligence, must at one time have possessed a simpler organization. Perhaps, at one time He was only what man is to-day. God, in "Mormon" theology, is the greatest intelligence; it will always remain the greatest; yet, it must of necessity, under the inexorable laws of the universe, grow. God is in no sense the Creator of natural forces and laws; He is the director of them.

God is the greatest intelligence.

The correct conclusion from this doctrine is that all the forces of nature are supported by intelligent action. This leads of necessity to order in nature. Blind forces, acting independently of intelligence, could not have brought about the perfect order that appears everywhere in the universe. Every atom of matter; every particle of ether is endowed with a form of intelligence. All the attractions, repulsions and equilibriums among natural objects are modes of expression of the force of intelligence. The explanations of the mysteries of nature will be greatly simplified when the "Mormon" doctrine of the position of intelligence in universal phenomena is clearly understood by scientific workers.

Since these teachings practically imply the definition that God is a superior intelligence evolved

Many grades of intelligence; hence, many Gods. from a lower condition, there can be no logical objection to the idea that there are many Gods. Yet, "Mormon" theology acknowledges the supremacy of the God of Abraham, Isaac, and Jacob. God transcends all human imagination. He is omniscient, and omnipotent; for His great knowledge enables Him to direct the forces of nature. He is full of love and mercy, because these qualities are attributes of intelligence, which God possesses in the highest degree. The "Mormon" idea of God, is delicate, refined, advanced and reasonable.

The interesting fact about this matter is, naturally, that in this conception of God, Joseph Smith was strictly scientific. He departed from the notion that God is a Being foreign to nature and wholly superior to it. Instead, he taught that God is part of nature, and superior to it only in the sense that the electrician is superior to the current that is transmitted along the wire. The great laws of nature are immutable, and even God can not transcend them.

This doctrine of God was taught by Joseph Smith early in his career. Can ignorance or disease produce such a logical climax of a scientific system of belief? Such a conclusion would be absurd.

Chapter XVIII.

JOSEPH SMITH'S EDUCATION.

Joseph Smith had few educational advantages during his life. His scientific teachings do not rest upon information gained in schools or from books. His parents fully appreciated the value of an education, but the pioneer lives which they led, and their numerous financial misfortunes, made it impossible for them to realize their desires for the education of their children. The Prophet's mother writes that when Joseph was about six years old, Hyrum, the elder brother, was sent to an academy at Hanover, New Hampshire, and the smaller children to a common school.* It is probable that throughout the wanderings of the family, the children were given such meager schooling as was possible. Joseph was a "remarkably quiet, well-disposed child," and his life up to the age of fourteen was marked only by those trivial circumstances which are common to childhood.†

A few months after his fourteenth birthday, the future prophet beheld his first vision. In his autobiography he mentions that at the time "he was doomed to the necessity of obtaining a scanty main-

Joseph Smith's early educational opportunities were very limited.

---

* History of the Prophet by his Mother, Improvement Era, Vol. 5, p. 166.

† Ibid p. 247.

tenance by his daily labor.''* This would indicate that at this age he was spending little or no time in school. During the time that elapsed between his fourteenth and eighteenth years, there is nothing to show that the boy was receiving scholastic education. The Prophet says that he was left to all kinds of temptation, and mingled with all kinds of society.† Nothing is said about the acquirement of book learning. About the age of nineteen he writes, ''As my father's worldly circumstances were very limited, we were under the necessity of laboring with our hands, hiring out by day's work and otherwise, as we could get opportunity. In the month of October, 1825, I hired with an old gentleman by the name of Josiah Stoal. During the time I was thus employed, I was put to board with a Mr. Isaac Hale—it was there I first saw my wife (his daughter), Emma Hale. On the 18th of January, 1827, [when the Prophet was a little more than twenty-one years old] we were married, while I was yet employed in the service of Mr. Stoal. Immediately after my marriage, I left Mr. Stoal's and went to my father's, and farmed with him that season.''‡ From his eighteenth to his twenty-second year, then, there is evidence that he worked as an ordinary laborer, and attended no school.

It seems, moreover, that Joseph Smith was not a boy to gather information from books, for his mother says of him, when he was eighteen years old, that ''he seemed much less inclined to the perusal of books than any of the rest of our children, but far more

---

* History of the Church, vol. 1, p. 7.   † Ibid p. 9.

‡ History of the Church, Vol. 1, pp. 16, 17.

given to meditation and deep study."* From the records extant, the conclusion is justifiable that from his fourteenth to his twenty-second year Joseph Smith received practically no school education, and did no extensive reading. What he might have gathered from conversation with others during that time is unknown to us. However, it is known that the heavenly messengers who visited him at intervals gave him much valuable information, which more than compensated for his poor scholastic advantages.

One month before his twenty-second birthday, the golden plates were delivered to the Prophet, and the next two and a half years he was engaged with various assistants in translating the Book of Mormon; though at different times during this period he farmed and did other manual labor. During this period (twenty-two to twenty-four and a half years of age), he most certainly attended no school nor gave special attention to worldly knowledge.

On the 6th of April, 1830, when the Prophet was twenty-four years and four months old, the Church was organized. The life led by the Prophet from this time to 1844, when he was assassinated, was not conducive to the gathering of information, and quiet, deep reflection. During almost the whole of this period his life was in danger; scores of times he was arrested on trumped-up charges; the Church was driven from place to place; he built at least three cities, and two temples; organized and governed the body of the Church; taught the doctrinal system ac-

* History of the Prophet Joseph, Improvement Era, Vol. 5, p. 257.

cepted by his followers; organized the public ministry of the Church for spreading the Gospel among all men, wrote his autobiography; compiled the revelations given him, and made a revision of parts of the Bible.

The mistake must not be made, however, of assuming that because the Prophet's education had

Joseph Smith taught the importance of schools and education.

been limited, he lacked a due appreciation of schools and scholastic attainments. On the contrary, at a very early date in the history of the Church, schools were organized even for the older men, that they might improve their time and make up in a manner for the lack of opportunity during their early days. During the winter of 1832-3, a school of the prophets was organized in Kirtland, Ohio, and another in Independence, Missouri, at which the elders of the Church received various instructions. In the discussion relative to the building of temples, references to schools being held in them were always made, and, in fact, in the fall of 1835, when a portion of the Kirtland temple was finished, "schools were opened in the various apartments." Many "were organized into a school for the purpose of studying the Hebrew language."[*] The reading of Greek had previously been begun. In these languages as well as in German, the Prophet acquired considerable facility. His studies tended, of course, towards the interpretation of the Bible and the explanation of Gospel truths; though at times his investigations appeared quite foreign to his special work, as when, in 1838, he began the methodical study of law.

---

* Autobiography of P. P. Pratt, p. 140.

When the city of Nauvoo was chartered, a section was included, providing for the establishment of a university, to be called the University of the City of Nauvoo, under the direction of which should be taught "all matters pertaining to education, from common schools up to the highest branches of a most liberal collegiate education."*

In numerous revelations did the Lord urge the Prophet and the Church to gather information from every source, of which the following quotations are good illustrations: "Teach ye diligently, that you may be instructed in theory, in principle, of things both in heaven and in the earth, and under the earth; things which have been, things which are, things which must shortly come to pass; things which are at home, things which are abroad; the wars and perplexities of the nations, and a knowledge also of countries and kingdoms. Seek ye out of the best books words of wisdom; seek learning even by study."† "Obtain a knowledge of history, and of countries and of kingdoms, of laws of God and man."‡ "Study and learn and become acquainted with all good books, and with languages, tongues and peoples."§ "It is imposible for a man to be saved in ignorance."‖ A more comprehensive outline of education can hardly be imagined. The energetic manner in which the Church has acted upon these instructions, during its whole history, need not be recounted here.

However much the Prophet sought for knowl-

---

* History of Joseph Smith, George Q. Cannon, pp. 341, 343.

† Doctrine and Covenants, 88: 78, 79, 118.

‡ Ibid 93: 53.   § Ibid 90: 15.   ‖ Ibid 131: 6.

edge, even from books, in his later life, the fact remains that the evidence in our possesion indicates that, up to the time of the organization of the Church, his book learning was very slight, and that during the years immediately following, his time was so fully occupied with the details of the organization that little or no time was given to education, as ordinarily understood. These statements are of especial importance, in view of the fact that all the principles discussed in this volume were enunciated before the end of the year 1833.

The associates of the Prophet are unanimous in saying that his spiritual and intellectual growth was **Though the Prophet had little book learning, the spirlual and intellectual growth was great.** marvelous, from the time that the work of the ministry fell upon him. He was transformed from a humble country lad to a leader among men, whose greatness was felt by all, whether unlearned or educated, small or great. Of himself the Prophet said, "I am a rough stone. The sound of the hammer and chisel was never heard on me until the Lord took me in hand. I desire the learning and wisdom of heaven alone." Certainly, his whole history shows that the great learning which he did manifest was acquired in a manner very different from that followed by the majority of men.

A SUMMARY RESTATEMENT OF PRINCIPLES.

Chapter XIX.

In its broadest sense, philosophy includes all that man may know of the universe—of himself and of the things about him. To be worthy of its name, a system of philosophy must possess certain comprehensive, fundamental principles, which if clearly understood, make intelligible to the human mind any or all of the phenomena in the universe. The simplier these foundation principles are, the greater is the system as a philosophy. In the words of Spencer, ''Philosophy is knowledge of the highest degree of generality,'' or ''completely unified knowledge.''*

It is to be observed, that the great laws of nature are inferred only from a number of lesser laws that have been gathered by man. A generalization which is not built upon numerous confirmatory observations, is at best an uncertain guess, which can be accepted only when demonstrated to be correct by numerous isolated experiences. The rational philosopher proceeds from the many to the few; he groups and groups again, until the wide, fundamental laws have been attained.

In olden days, and at times today, this method was not pursued. A philosopher, so called, would assume that a certain statement or idea were true. Upon this idea an elaborate, speculative, philoso-

Philosophy and its methods.

---

* First Principles, pp. 133 and 136.

phical superstructure was reared. If by chance, and the chance usually came, the fundamental notion were shown to be false, the whole system fell with a crash into the domain of untruth.

It is the 'glory of modern science that by its methods, innumerable facts, correct so far as present instruments and man's senses will allow, have been gathered; and, that present day philosophy is built upon these certain facts. The errors, if any exist, of this philosophy lie not in the foundation stones, but in the inferences that have been drawn from them. Modern philosophy rests upon the truths of the universe, and not upon the wild speculations of men.

The philosophy of science, which is the basis of all rational philosophy, rests upon the doctrine of the

The fundamental conceptions of scientific philosophy. indestructibility of matter. Matter cannot be destroyed, and it is unthinkable that it ever was created. True, matter may appear in various forms: the tangible coal may escape through the chimneys as an intangible gas; water may vanish into vapor; gold may unite with acids to form compounds entirely unlike gold. However, the weight of the coal in the gases passing through the chimney is the same as the weight of the coal fed into the stove; the water vapor in the air weighs precisely as much as the water that was in the vessel; the gold in the compound weighs the same as the metallic gold used; in every case matter has been changed into another form, but has not been destroyed.

Along with this fundamental principle, science holds the doctrine of the indestructibility of energy. Matter of itself is dead and useless; it is only when it is in motion or in the possession of energy that it can take part in the processes of nature. Matter without energy is not known to man; however inert it may be, it possesses some energy." The ultimate particles of all things,—rock and plant, and beast and man—are in motion; that is, they possess energy. The immediate source of energy for this earth is the sun, though the ultimate source of universal energy is not known.

Energy may appear in varous forms, as light, heat, electricity, magnetism, gravitation and mechanical motion; and each of these forms of energy may be changed into any of the others. In every change, however, there is no loss, but simply a change of condition. That which men call energy, the vivifying principle of matter, is indestructible. It has never had a beginning, and shall never have an end.

To the mind of man, however, a motion independent of something in motion, is inconceivable. An ocean wave without water is nonsense. It is equally difficult to conceive of energy which is immaterial, passing from the sun to the earth, through empty space. There must be something between the earth and the sun, which carries the energy. Such reflections have led the thinkers to the belief that all space is filled with a subtle medium, now called the ether, through which energy passes in the form of waves. Today, few doctrines of science are so well established as that of the universal ether. The ether is a refined kind of matter which fills all space, and permeates all things. It is in the table on which I write; in and through the ink; between the ultimate particles of the glass of the ink bottle. This earth, and all heavenly bodies, are simply suspended in the all-and-ever-present ocean of ether. By the agency of the ether, energy is carried from the sun to the earth, and may be carried anywhere in space. Light, heat, electricity, magnetism and gravitation are all various manifestations of ether motion. Many scientists believe that this world—ether is the original matter from which the various elements have been made.

On these three doctrines, the indestructibility of matter, the indestructibility of energy, and the existence of the universal ether, rest primarily the explanations of the phenomena of nature. Hand in hand they stand, an almost perfect example of the greatness of the human mind.

The religion founded by Joseph Smith rests upon the same or similar laws. To the very beginner in "Mormon" theology, it is a familiar fact that Joseph Smith taught that matter is eternal, and has not been nor can be created. Matter is coexistent with God. God, himself, is material, in the sense that His body is composed of a refined kind of matter. In the fundamental laws that underlie all nature, there is perfect harmony between science and "Mormonism." Few religions can say as much. In most systems of theology, it is asumed that the ruling power, God, can create matter. In "Mormon" theology he can only organize it.

"Mormonism" and science have the same fundamental laws.

It is not quite so well understood that the doctrine of the indestructibility of energy lies also at the foundation of "Mormon" theology, and was taught by Joseph Smith. It was clearly comprehended by the Prophet and his associates that intelligence is the vivifying force of all creation—animate or inanimate—that rock and tree and beast and man, have ascending degrees of intelligence. The intelligence spoken of by the Prophet corresponds fully with the energy of science.

That the Prophet did not use the word current among scientific men at that time does not destroy the validity of this claim. Different words have no quarrel when they mean the same.

The Prophet also taught that this intelligence fills all space, and that it may appear in various forms, such as heat, light, and electricity, and that it is eternal, and can neither be created nor destroyed. These are the very qualities assigned to energy by scientific workers. This doctrine and its coincidence with the doctrine of science appears marvelous, when it is recalled that the Prophet laid down these teachings in 1831, more than ten years before they were discovered by scientists, and a generation before they were generally accepted by the scientific world.

The Prophet did not stop with the enunciation of these two fundamental doctrines. He declared that a refined medium, called the Holy Spirit, fills all space, whereby intelligence is conveyed from place to place. In the terms of Joseph Smith, the forces of nature, such as heat, light and electricity, are simply various manifestations of the intelligence of the Holy Spirit; in the terms of science, of the energy of the universal ether. The parallelism is complete. The Holy Spirit, in ''Mormon'' theology, corresponds with the ether of science. This doctrine, too, was enunciated many years before the corresponding doctrines were established among men of science.

The Prophet also taught the unchanging relation of cause and effect, which brings the whole **Cause** universe under a reign of law, and **and effect.** overthrows the mysticisms of old. This doctrine was emphasized at a time when the world was just beginning to insist upon it. He further taught clearly the manner in which nature's laws may be discovered by man.

The Prophet further taught that all the heavenly bodies are in motion; that the solar system is but a **Astronomy.** small part of a greater and grander whole, controlled by the same laws, and that some of these other worlds are inhabited. These doctrines, which now form the foundation of the new astronomy, was discovered and acepted by the world of science after the days of Joseph Smith.

He also held clear and modern views regarding **Geology.** time limits in geology, or the prehistoric ages of the world, at a time when students were not agreed on the subject.

Moreover, the ''Mormon'' prophet declared that the living beings found on earth were organized from **The in-** the commonly occurring elements and **dividual.** forces of nature in such a manner that through them the force of intelligence might exert itself in the greatest degree. Hence the individual is only an organized intelligence. This, too, is in perfect harmony with the results of the latest scholarship.

On the basis of the fundamental laws, above defined, what does science require of its devotees?

The laws for the individual. How does it affect the actions of the individual? As in theology, the scientific worker must have faith in the principles that have been discovered. It is not possible in one lifetime for a man to repeat all the work of preceding workers, to demonstrate the accuracy of their results. Much must be taken on trust; though at any time, should it be necessary, the earlier work may be repeated. Besides requiring faith in the principles discovered and enunciated by others, science demands that its every worker shall believe in things that lie far beyond the reach of man's senses.

In theology, at least in the system established by Joseph Smith, a similar faith is required of the individual. God and angels have been seen by very few individuals. These realities must be accepted by faith. In the words of the Prophet Joseph, "Faith is the assurance which men have of the existence of things which they have not seen, and the principle of action in all intelligent beings." With respect to the first principle of science and theology, "Mormonism" is in entire accord with the best philosophy. The individual, whether scientist or theologian, must base his work on faith.

The scientist who has acquired faith in a law of nature will no longer transgress that law. He will obey it. If he establishes the faith that a wire connected in a certain way with the electric dynamo carries a current sufficiently strong to destroy life, he will not wantonly seize that wire in his hands. Before this faith came to him, he probably came near losing his life, by the careless handling of the charged wire. To conform to the laws of nature is scientific repentance. Faith in science or religion is a high form of intelligence and is opposed to ignorance. Repentance is the use of this intelligence for the benefit of man.

In "Mormonism" the second principle of action for the individual is repentance. If faith in God has been attained and his laws have been made clear, the believer will no longer violate those laws; he will obey them. That is repentance. Not by a jot or tittle does this kind of repentance differ from the repentance taught by science. True, science does not *speak* of repentance, but it *thinks* it. In the matter of the great principle of repentance, governing the the action of workers in science or theology, "Mormonism" is eminently sane and philosophical. Faith does not compel men to repent; but it is a necessary precedent. The man who does not repent in science or theology, after he has acquired faith, renders himself liable to injury and retards his own progress.

In the system of theology taught by Joseph Smith, baptism is the third great principle to be obeyed by the individual; that is, unless baptism follows faith and repentance it is impossible to enter the kingdom of God. In science there is a counterpart of baptism which is the third principle of scientific progress.

A man who has attained faith in electricity resolves to refrain from violating any of the laws of electricity. If he desires to produce a current of electricity, he winds a wire around a piece of iron, and revolves the coil in the field of a magnet, and the curernt is produced. If the wire has not been wound in a certain definite manner, and has not been placed in the proper relation to the magnet, no current can be produced. The scientist may rail and object that it is all nonsense to insist that the work be done just so to produce the current. Nature is inexorable. The man to enter the kingdom of the electric current must yield obedience to the order of nature; he *must receive a scientific baptism.*

The baptism taught by the theology of Joseph Smith is nothing more than obedience to law. Just why it is necessary to be buried in the water to enter the Church, perhaps no man fully knows. Nor does any one know just *why* the wire must be wound, just so, to produce the current of electricity. Of one thing every thinker may be certain, that the essential principle of baptism is as necessary in science as in theology. In this matter also, then, Joseph the Prophet is eminently philosophical.

The fourth principle in "Mormon" theology teaches that after baptism, the gift of the Holy Ghost is conferred which enlightens the mind, clears the intelligence, and brings man nearer the presence of God. So also in science, to the man who obeys the law of nature, come greater power and intelligence, to him who winds the wire right, the electric current comes, with all its latent powers. Thus is the Holy Ghost conferred in science; and thus, also, in a more subtle and greater degree is it conferred in the Church. The dogma of Joseph Smith and the teachings of science harmonize perfectly in the examination of the fourth fundamental principle of the philosophy governing the individual.

It is becoming fairly well demonstrated that the ceaseless changes and transformations in nature cause a greater and greater complexity in nature.

Evolution. This, in other words, means that the earth and all on it are developing and progressing. According to Darwin and his followers, man and animals advance. Only those who progress, persist; those who retrograde, die. Creation as a whole grows and develops, and must of necessity do so. By this law, the purpose of the earth and the universe is explained to be endless growth. The law of evolution is the great cementing law of science. Even so, in the philosophy of Joseph Smith, the doctrine is taught that all things advance; that man shall continue to advance, in intelligence, and all pertaining to it, until he shall become as God is now. Meanwhile, our God will also increase in his fulness, and ever be a God to us. Through this dictrine, all the principles of the Gospel are made coherent. All the requirements of man have in view his eternal growth. Man's presence here on earth is simply that he may better learn to understand the nature of gross matter; and thus to develop and progress more completely.

It is remarkable that Joseph Smith taught the law of evolution as an eternal truth, twenty or more years before Darwin published his views.

Above the law of laws is the force of forces—or the central force of the universe. Science has little to say

God. of God. It is content to accept the laws of nature as they are found. Yet, at times, in some branches of science, a knowledge of the beginning of things is desired. Usually science answers, " I do not know;'' but it nevertheless affirms that there must be a central force, unknown and unnamed, to which the manifestations of all other forces may be referred. Science, which is essentially orderly, is chaotic when the question of the beginning of things is raised. The ''Mormon'' Prophet left no such weakness in his philosophy. He, too, realized the necessity of a controlling universal force. This he named God. God is an organized, material being, filled with the form of energy known as intelligence. ''The glory of God is intelligence.'' All other forces of nature may be converted into intelligence; and from intelligence all other forces may be obtained; God is the center of these forces, and their directing power. Because of this centralization, nature is orderly. Natrual laws are not, as supposed by some philosophers, accidental relations of phenomena, observed and recorded by man. The force of intelligence controls all phenomena; there is mind behind the operations of nature. God, himself a part of nature, is not the creator of nature, but the organizer and director of it. What a beautifully reasonable climax that is to the wonderful philosophy of Joseph the Prophet!

The intelligence of God is organized; therein lies his individuality and life. Man is organized intelligence; therein lies his life. Through obedience to law, intelligence grows; by the violation of law, which is sin, it decays. It is the degree of organized intelligence that ultimately distinguishes one man from other men; men from beasts, beasts from plants, and plants from rocks. Since intelligence, as defined by Joseph Smith, corresponds with the main form of energy of the universe, the doctrine of God, and all

other beings, and of life, finds expresison in terms
of energy. That is exactly what science demands.

Is it any wonder that workers in science, who
have been taught the doctrine of an immaterial God
Theology and   who is able to create something from
science agree.   nothing, and to transcend all laws of
nature, depart from the faith of their childhood?
Truth is truth forever. Scientific truth cannot be
theological lie.   To the sane mind, theology and
philosophy must harmonize. They have the common
ground of truth on which to meet.

Thus, on every hand, from the highest to the
lowest, from the force of forces and the law of laws
to the fundamental laws governing the operations of
the universe, and the actions of the individual, the
philosophy of the "Mormon" Prophet is consistently
referred back to matter, energy and law.   In its
completeness, it transcends the philosophy of science.
Wherever the doctrines of "Mormonism" and
science meet, they agree. No discord has yet been
found between them. Science is daily confirming
the truth of the universe—embracing philosophy of
the unlearned founder of "Mormonism."

Back of the revelations of the greatness of the
Prophet's knowledge that come to all who enter
upon such a discussion, stands the eminent fact that
"Mormon" philosophy is plain, simple, and easily
understood. There is no need and no room for mysteries in the teachings of Joseph the Prophet. Similarly, the philosophy of men, based upon nature, is
essentially simple, and easily understood. Only untruth needs to hide itself in mysteries.

One hundred years have passed since Joseph, honored and chosen of God, entered the school of life. Face to face with God, Joseph learned the Gospel, planned before the foundations of the world were laid, and he taught it to a careless world. It is not Joseph Smith's philosophy; but God's code of fundamental laws, which the world is laboriously deciphering in the beautifully written pages of nature. Is it any wonder that the philosophy is perfect?

Of simple brilliancy must have been the mind of the Prophet which was able to discover in the forgotten corners of thought the priceless gems of controlling, universal truth.

Chapter XX.

CONCLUDING THOUGHTS.

It has been shown in the preceding chapters that Joseph Smith recognized and stated the fundamental laws of all science, the fundamental principles of physical and biological science and astronomy, together with a great number of scientific facts, and made these statements usually in advance of workers in science.

It is a surprising fact that a young man of twenty-eight, who had had no educational advantages of schooling, or reading, or society, should state clearly and correctly known laws of science; but it is marvelous that he should state fundamental laws that the workers in science did not discover until many years later. Every honest man, be he friend or enemy, must marvel, and ask, "Whence did this man derive his knowledge?"

Was he a man of lively imagination who gussed shrewdly? If so, he was the shrewdest guesser the world has known. All that he said has come true; his bitterest enemies have been unable to prove incorrect statements of facts. Their attacks have always been on the origin of the work, on its ethical ideals (which are largely personal opinions), and on the probability that Joseph Smith was the real founder of "Mormonism"—thus tacitly admitting the greatness of the work. Had he been a guesser, simply, he would have failed somewhere, and thus revealed his weakness. But let any man show one error in the inspired writings of Joseph Smith, even when he dealt with matters which lay far outside of his daily mission. Though thousands of persons have felt impelled to war against "Mormonism," no such error has been found. All human logic denies that he was a guesser.

Did he receive his knowledge from well educated persons, who kept themselves in the background? No documentary evidence has been found to substantiate such a view. Primarily, it is unlikely that men of intelligence and education would hide behind an ignorant boy, from the time he was fourteen until his death at thirty-nine years of age. There was nothing to gain by it; the prophet never had more wealth than just enough to live on; the pleasure that his power over his followers gave him, was more than offset by the ceaseless persecution which followed him. Besides, nearly all the fairly well educated men who joined the Church in the early days were given prominent positions in the Church, yet it is known that they were instructed or chastised by the youthful prophet whenever occasion required, as were those of no or little education. Joseph Smith was always greater than any of his followers. But above all, no educated man would have been able to tell Joseph, by means of his education, of things not yet known. The idea that Joseph Smith was only a dummy for clever heads is not tenable.

Since ordinary means were beyond his power, how did he acquire his knowledge? How was he able to look into the future, and reveal its secrets?

"Ah," says a new philosopher, "I have it, he was epileptic, and had trances, during which his visions appeared;" and the philosopher proceeds to write a book proving his theory to be correct.* What a pitiful attempt to push the question into the region of the unknown; and at the same time, what a splendid acknowledgment of the fact that the life and labors of Joseph Smith transcend ordinary human explanations! Do epileptics, in their phantasms, see orderly systems of truth, which are carried into effect in their days of health and sanity? Does the epiletptic see the truth that shall be revealed in the coming ages, and teach it with a stately soberness of language which admits of no uncertainty? If so, then might the race well long for the time when the great gift of healthful, reasoning imagination shall be exchanged for the ghastly disease of epilepsy. Folly of follies! The life, writings and works of Joseph Smith are healthy, above all else; no trace of physical, or mental, or spiritual disease can be found in them. His teachings are given as eternal truths revealed by the God of nature; and they rise loftily above the vague theorizings of the investigator, or the uncertain gibberish of the diseased intellect. Clearness, reason, logic in method and execution, characterize the teachings and works of Joseph Smith. Have such qualities ever indicated disease?

To the person who can rise above his prejudices, and confess to himself that he is not able to explain in the manner of men how Joseph Smith came by his knowledge of ideas, men and things, comes the

---

* The Founder of Mormonism. Riley.

strong conviction that the "Mormon" prophet was inspired by a mightier power than men possess; and if that conviction is followed by a prayerful desire to know what that power is, the testimony will be given that from God, the Controller of the universe, known by various men under divers names, did Joseph Smith receive, directly, the truths which fill the pages of his published writings, and direct the lives of his followers.

God spoke to Joseph, and gave him the revelations necessary for building his kingdom in the last days. Little more than was necessary did the Lord reveal, but occasionally, for the comfort of the prophet and his associates, truths were given which hinted of the glorious order of the universe. May it not be, also, that the Lord showed Joseph many truths, similar to those touched upon in these papers, in order that later generations might have additional testimonies of the divinity of the latter-day work? Under the influence of the Holy Spirit, the boy Joseph grew into a man, whose mind was filled with the great vision of the contents and the destiny of the universe, including the future lot of mankind. No man has had a nobler education than that received by Joseph Smith.

When the historian of future days shall review the history of the growth of science, and shall judge men by the record that they have left behind them, he will place Joseph Smith as the greatest philosopher of science of the nineteenth century, and possibly of the twentieth. Then will men reverently speak of that mighty mind and clear vision, which, inspired by the God of heaven, saw, as in an open book, the truths which men have later developed, through ceaseless labor and countless vigils. Then shall the thinkers of the future speak of him as Joseph, the clearsighted.

Knowledge, concentrated into wisdom, is the end of existence. To those who live according to God's law, knowledge will come easily. It will continue to come to his people, until it shall be the most intelligent among the nations. The Lord has said it.

"How long can rolling waters remain impure? What power shall stay the heavens? As well might man stretch forth his puny arm to stop the Missouri River in its decreed course, or turn it up stream, as to hinder the Almighty from pouring down knowledge from heaven upon the heads of the Latter-day Saints."*

---

* Doctrine and Covenants, 121: 33.

Chapter XXI.

A VOICE FROM THE SOIL.

I.

"——the defenced city shall be desolate, and the habitation forsaken, and left like a wilderness."
—*Isaiah, xxvii:* 10.

It is a fact, which has impressed itself upon all readers of history, that countries which have been the homes of the most powerful and cultured nations, are now great stretches of the veriest desert. No country teaches this truth better than the extensive valley of the Mesopotamia which looms giant-like in the dawn of history. Upon its plains and highlands, the great nations of antiquity acted the tragedies of their existence; like the schoolboys' snowman, they rose, with vast proportions, in a day, and fell ere the setting of the next sun. In this district, advanced and retreated with wonderful precision, as it appears to us so many ages removed from the time of action, the Chaldeans, the Babylonians and the Assyrians; here the Medes and Persians achieved the victories that made them famous, and here came all the great generals of old to crown their successes. A hundred populous cities clustered, in the lower part of the valley, around Babylon the great, the most marvelous city of any past age; a hundred cities were in the upper half, with Nineveh, also magnificent and great, as their center. From Mesopotamia come evidences of art—painting, sculpture, music, literature and architecture—the indication of a higher civilization. Still, today, even the sites of many of the great cities are lost, and Mesopotamia is a stretch of barren land.

To the west of Mesopotamia is the valley containing the promised land of Palestine—it, also, has fallen from its former splendor, and is a desert compared with the days of its greatest prosperity. Still further west and south lies the land of Egypt, in the valley of the Nile. It was the fostermother of science, and the shaker of empires. It has fallen likewise; and a blight has come upon the soil, until it bears the appearance of a sandy waste. Over the sites of other famous nations of antiquity, in Europe and Asia, hovers, today, the spirit of desolation.

The same story is told on the American continent. Peru, the land of the Incas, once populous, powerful, wealthy, is today largely a wilderness. Mexico, the Aztec home, is now a vast desert, in spite of the evidence, through the discovered ruins of mighty cities and gigantic temples, that it was once the home of a strong people. Central America tells a similar story. It seems to be a general fact that wherever a large people lived formerly, there, today, a desert often occurs.

However, these countries are deserts only because human effort is no longer applied to them; by proper treatment the lands would again be raised to the flourishing condition that prevailed in their prosperous days. Intrinsically the soils are extremely fertile, but are dry and require the application of water to make the fertility suitable for the use of crops. The soils of Babylon, Assyria, Egypt, Peru and Mexico, raise crops of wonderful yields when properly irrigated; and there is abundant proof that in former days irrigation was practiced in these countries on a scale far larger than in Utah or in any other country of the present day.

Many of the old irrigation canals of Babylon still exist, and prove the magnitude of the practice, there, of the art of irrigation. The old historians, also, agree in explaining the ingenious devices by which whole rivers were turned from their courses to flow over the soil. In Egypt, likewise, irrigation was more commonly practiced in the past than it is today; though even now a large portion of the soil of that country is made to yield crops by the artificial application of water. In Peru, Central America, and Mexico, the irrigation canals that remain from prehistoric days are even more wonderful as feats of engineering and as evidences of a populous and enlightened condition of the country than the massive temples and extensive cities that are also found. In the construction of these canals every precaution, apparently, was taken to have the water applied to the lands in the right manner, and to reduce the loss to a minimum. In some places immense canals remain, that are tiled for miles, on sides and bottom, in order to render them watertight, and thus prevent any loss by seepage.

Instead of saying, then, that the countries where most great nations have lived are now deserts, we may as well say that most great nations have lived in countries where irrigation was necessary; in fact, that history indicates that a dense population, and high culture, usually go hand in hand with a soil that thirsts for water. What can science, the great explainer, say on this subject?

II.

"Science moves, but slowly, slowly, moving on from point to point."—*Locksley Hall.*

A plant feeds in two ways—by its leaves, and by its roots. The leaves feed from the air; the roots from the soil. In the air is found a colorless, heavy gas, known as carbon dioxide, which is made up partly of the element of carbon, or charcoal. When an animal or a plant is burned at a low heat, it first chars, showing the presence of charcoal; then if the burning be continued, it disappears, with the exception of the ash, as the gas, carbon dioxide. Since animal and vegetable matters are constantly being burned upon the earth's surface, naturally the air contains a perceptible quantity of carbon dioxide. The leaves of a living plant, waving back and forth, draw into themselves the carbon dioxide with which they come into contact, and there break it up and take the carbon away from it. The carbon thus obtained by the leaves is built into the many ingredients of a plant, and carried to the parts that are in greatest need. The plant is able to do this by virtue of the peculiar properties of the green coloring matter in all its leaves, leaf green; which acts, however, only in the presence of bright sunlight. Since one-half or more of the dry matter of a plant is carbon, the importance of the leaf-air-feeding of a plant may be understood.

The water which a plant contains and the incombustible portions, the mineral matters or ash, are taken directly from the soil by means of the roots. The old idea that vegetable mould and other corbonaceous matters are also taken from the soil by the roots has been shown to be erroneous. The mineral portions of a plant are of the highest value to the life of the plant—without them, in fact, it languishes and dies. If a soil on which a plant is growing contains, for instance, no iron, the leaves become pale, soon white, and finally they lose the power of appropriating carbon from the air. If potash is absent from the soil, the plants growing upon it will develop in an imperfect manner and finally die. It has been found by careful experiment that seven mineral substances must be found in every soil, if it shall support the life of plants, namely: (1) Potash; (2) lime; (3) magnesia; (4) oxide of iron or iron rust; (5) sulphuric acid or oil of vitriol; (6, phosophoric acid, and (7) nitric acid or aqua fortis. The fertility of any soil or soil district is determined by the quantity of these indispensable ash ingredients contained by it.

All soils are produced by the breaking down of the mountains under the influence of weathering. The broken down rock is washed into the hollows and lowlands by the rains and floods of melted snow, and there forms soil. Soil may, therefore, be defined, in a general way, as pulverized rock. Nearly all rocks contain the elements above enumerated as being essential to a plant's life; and nearly every soil will, consequently, be in possession of them. Rocks, however, in being subjected to the action of weathering, undergo other changes than mere pulverization. The potash, lime and other plant foods held by a rock are in an insoluble condition, and can not be taken up with any ease by the plant roots. As the rock is pulverized in the process of weathering, it is also made more soluble, and the juices of the plant roots can then absorb the needed foods with greater facility. This process of making the soil more soluble, continues while time lasts, and every year will find the soil more soluble than the year before, if there are no opposing actions. Therefore, the fertility of a soil is determined not only by the quantity of plant food it contains, but also by the condition of solubility the soil constituents are in.

According to the facts above given, it would be fair to infer that a soil becomes more fertile with every year that passes. This would be the case were it not for opposing tendencies. First, the crops grown upon a soil remove considerable quantities of mineral plant food. This alone would not seriously affect the fertility of a soil did not other forces act in conjunction with it. The most important cause of lowering the fertility of soils is the loss of plant food due to drainage. In districts of abundant rainfall, as, for instance, the Eastern United States, sufficient rain falls to soak the soil thoroughly and to drain through and go off as drainage water. The water, in passing through the soil, will dissolve, as far as it can, the soluble ingredients, including the plant foods, and carry them away into the rivers and finally into the ocean. This action, continued for many years, will rob the soil to feed the ocean; in fact, the saltness of the ocean is due, largely, to the substances washed out of the soils. Most of the poor soils of the world have been rendered infertile in this way. If, on the other hand, only a small quantity of rain falls upon the soil—an amount sufficient to soak the soil without draining through—the water will gradually be evaporated back into the air, and there will be no loss of plant food. In such a district the soils, if they are treated right, become richer year by year, even though subjected to tillage, if the tillage be according to our best knowledge.

In every rainless district, or in every district where the rainfall is so slight as to render irrigation necessary, the soils would be expected to be richer than in a place of abundant rainfall. Leaving out of consideration differences due to local conditions, this has been verified by the study of soils from many parts of the world. The soils of an arid district contain more soluble plant food than those of a humid district, and, with proper treatment, will not only raise larger crops, but remain fertile much longer. They will also bear harsher treatment, closer cultivation, and are in every respect superior to the water-washed soils of a humid country. A recent study of the soils of Utah has shown that the fertility of our soils is exceedingly high, and that they will endure long and close cultivation; that is, that because of the peculiar climatic conditions of the State, they can support bountifully a large population.

Several years ago Dr. E. W. Hilgard, an eminent student of climate and soils, threw out the suggestion that upon the facts just discussed rests the explanation of the historical datum that the great nations of antiquity on this and on other continents sought for the abodes the rainless, arid stretches of the world. A large, active population, which does not depend on other peoples for its support, must of necessity possess the most fertile lands, which are found only in districts of limited rainfall. In the whole history of the world, the great granaries of the world have been located on the arid stretches; and on our continent, the great West, largely arid, is becoming the source of the food staples of the nation. Utah is the heart of the arid region of North America; her soils are heavy with wealth of plant food. If the time comes that her valleys be filled with people, crowding in from the nations of the earth, her soils, responding to the better treatment which science is developing day by day, will display their strength, and feed the world, should the demand be made.

III.

"Therefore will I make solitary places to bud and blossom, and to bring forth in abundance, saith the Lord."—*Doctrine and Covenants.*

Sixty years ago the facts of plant feeding, as just outlined, were practically unknown. The erroneous ideas of the preceding century still held full sway. In 1840 Liebig published his treatise on agricultural chemistry which threw a faint light on the relation of the plant and the soil. During the twenty years following, the indispensable nature of some of the plant foods was ascertained; and it is only within the last ten or fifteen years that the superiority of arid districts over humid ones, for the purpose of supporting man, has been demonstrated. Even today it is a new light which has not been fully received.

In 1842 Joseph the Prophet wrote: "I prophesied that the saints would continue to suffer much affliction and would be driven to the Rocky Mountains * * * and some of you will live to go and assist in making settlements and build cities and see the saints become a mighty people in the midst of the Rocky Mountains." Why did Joseph Smith speak of the Rocky Mountains as a gathering place for his people? Was it simply because the place was far off and offered, apparently, good security? If so, he builded better than he knew. But what prompted Brigham Young to plant his cane by the shore of an alkali lake and say, Here we shall remain? That certainly was not for security only. Perhaps he was tired of wandering? Though he may have been so, yet he was not the man to give up when near something better. Perhaps he thought the valley fair, and the blue mountains may have rested his eyes? If that was the motive of settlement, he, too, builded better than he knew. Certainly it is that these two men who historically hold the responsibility for bringing the Latter-day Saints here, did not know, by the world's learning, that the valleys of Utah are filled with the richest soil, waiting only to yield manifold to the husbandman; for the world did not yet know, and had no means for predicting it. These men were not scientists. They had no laboratories in which, by long hours, over long drawn fires, and among a hundred fumes, to draw out for themselves the law of the fertility of arid soils, which has but recently become the property of modern science. It is not likely that the records of a lost learning, unknown today, taught them this fact. Though they had had such records, they were unlettered men, and the ancient tongues would have been dead indeed to them, had they attempted an interpretation by their own efforts. Why then, did they bring the people here? Was it a chance move? A blind effort, acting out the desperation that comes from long persecution? If an element of chance entered into the location in the valleys of Utah, it was akin to wisdom.

And it was wisdom of the highest kind; at which the world ever stands in reverent wonder; inspiration from the living God. The logic that science, itself, applies to facts in the deduction of its laws, makes it impossible to believe that the settlement of the pioneers in the Salt Lake Valley was a chance move. Nothing, from the point of view of human wisdom, encouraged the pioneers to remain in Utah— they were in the center of a desert; the leaders were urged by many of the company to go on, for there were fairer climes to the west or the south, or on the islands of the sea. But the leaders were possessed of a wisdom higher than that of men, and founded an empire on the wastes of the Great American Desert.

Now, let every reader of this paper consider these wonderful facts: Of the vast possibilities of agriculture in Utah being the same with those of the countries where the great nations of the world have lived; of a people, claiming that the nations shall in the future flee to it for safety, making its home in a place which possesses the capabilities of supporting the nations; and of the choice of that country when it was named a desert; when science, the world's knowledge, did not dream of the fertility of that desert any more than it was able to give a correct explanation of the fertility of the valley of Mesopotamia: and every honest heart will recognize the unseen hand of the God of Israel, guiding the people of God to the destined land.